SPELL STRUCK
MIDLIFE SPELL HUNTER BOOK TWO

AMY BOYLES

LADYBUGBOOKS LLC

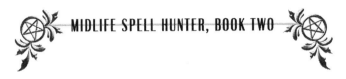

MIDLIFE SPELL HUNTER, BOOK TWO

Spell Struck

Amy Boyles

CHAPTER 1

"What are you doing?" Georgia hissed.

"I'm trying to stay behind you so that we don't get separated," Dane snapped.

"Just stay close and we won't."

"In case you hadn't noticed, it's dark in here."

It was dark, inky dark in fact. The old factory that Georgia and Dane were in, though it had plenty of broken windows on the surface, was pitch-black in the basement, where they currently resided. Well, *resided* might not be the right word. If one called residing splashing through tunnels with an inch of water in them as rats the size of cantaloupes scurried by, residing it was.

But Georgia did not refer to that as *residing*. The closest phrase she could come to describe her current situation was *dumpster diving*.

And that was being kind.

From behind her, Dane huffed. "Why don't you let me get in front?"

"Because I have a better sense of direction than you."

"You just don't want to let me because I'm your husband and you always feel a need to be in charge."

This was true. Georgia did indeed have a desire to be the person leading the force. It came from a past life of being a spell hunter. Well, that wasn't just her *past* life—it was her current one as well.

Georgia had retired from spell hunting when she married Dane. Not only that, but she'd given up her powers of witchcraft as well—all for the sake of a man she believed to be mortal, human.

As it turned out, her humdrum life in the suburbs became a bit too humdrum. Feeling underappreciated by her husband and being the only forty-five-year-old mom with a kindergartener took their toll on Georgia, so after a visit from her former employer and mentor, Georgia called on the goddess to return her powers. The goddess, being a kind and giving deity, gave Georgia what she asked for.

So she re-enlisted as a spell hunter again, and wound up confronting another spell hunter who turned out to be—Dane! Her husband, all along, had been a wizard who, it turned out, didn't work at a regular nine-to-five. No. Dane was a spell hunter, same as she had been.

After a lengthy battle in which the two of them nearly destroyed their home (okay, mostly Georgia), they rediscovered the sizzle in their marriage and decided to team up to seek out the mind-control spell that they'd each been hired to find.

They found the spell, realized that the people who claimed to be their allies were not, and decided to go into business together.

Which was how Dane and Georgia found themselves in the basement of an abandoned factory investigating a tip that hidden beneath was a stash of spells—among them a weakness spell that was so strong it could cripple a person. It was the type of magic that shouldn't get into the wrong hands. It was the sort of spell that could put people in the hospital.

Georgia didn't know what the evil wizard who'd acquired the power wanted it for. All she knew was that the spell was here and the wizard who owned it? Well, she'd had a run-in with him years ago. He was the sort of fella who always stayed in trouble and yet who also happened to keep the same hunting grounds—those near Huntsville, Alabama.

She'd always thought it strange that a wizard or even a witch, with the unlimited resources that magic offered, would stay in smaller towns or cities. Why not move someplace huge where one could disappear?

Well, it didn't matter, she guessed. Because even though Donalbain wasn't technically in any trouble for having the spell (it wasn't illegal to keep a spell of weakness in one's possession), all that did matter was plucking it from his possession and storing it away someplace safe.

The man did not have a good reputation. Simply put, he couldn't be trusted with such magic.

Dane's voice came clipped behind her. "You're blocking the tunnel." He certainly was testy on this run. "I can't see up ahead."

"It's dark." She flipped her head and ponytail over her shoulder to look at him. "There's not much to see."

"I would like to know that myself."

She stopped, annoyed, and released a deep breath. "Look, you and me—we're supposed to be a team. Remember? A team."

"We are a team."

He stared at her through his night-vision goggles. Dane had insisted they bring them even though they could have just as simply used magic to light their way. But with the goggles on, there was less chance that they'd be spotted by anyone.

As if a gaggle of people wanted to hang out in a sewer-stinking, rat-infested tunnel that wound beneath a factory. Georgia was pretty sure that the only thing they would end up finding was a stack of bones and a sewer monster intent on devouring them. Maybe an alien.

Maybe both.

Dane spoke in that husky voice of his that even after ten years still made her stomach clench. "I just want to keep you safe. Do you mind if I go first?"

He wouldn't be happy until he was in front. So Georgia sighed heavily and stepped back, gesturing for him to take the lead. "Be my guest."

As he passed her, Dane paused to plant a kiss on her lips. "This doesn't mean that I don't think you're in charge."

"Right."

"You're in charge in the bedroom."

"And I wouldn't have it any other way." She had to stop herself from wrapping her fingers around his neck and entwining them in his hair that was streaked here and there with gray. "Now, let's get that spell and get out of here."

His fingers grazed her rump, and Georgia shifted uncomfortably. Yes, she'd been training with Dane. Yes, she'd been working out. But by goodness, the fat on her thighs and rear end had moved in and threatened to never leave. It was like as soon as she hit forty, her body revolted on her. It no longer snapped back into shape after a few weeks of exercise and dieting. In fact, her body refused to lose weight. The fat hung out like an unwelcome guest. The only way to get rid of it was to either cut it off or…cut it off.

Neither of which sounded like good ideas to her.

But she pushed the thoughts of her traitorous body from her mind as Dane led them down the path, their accessories jangling. They both wore all black and had ammunition belts draped over their shoulders.

No, these belts didn't hold bullets. Instead they secured spells to their wearers. Georgia counted at least twenty on her. They did everything from cloaking, making her invisible, to turning anyone attacking her into a giant blueberry, à la *Willy Wonka and the Chocolate Factory*.

"Because they'll never expect it," Dane had said with a note of pride when she asked him why he'd given her that spell.

She couldn't agree more. No perpetrator would expect to be fighting one moment and blowing up into a fruit the next.

That much was certain.

Brad's voice crackled over the headsets both of them wore. "You're going to reach a fork in the tunnels in about ten feet. Take a right."

"Copy that," Dane said.

"Georgia, you still leading the way?" Brad asked.

She pressed down a button to talk. "No, my husband forced me to take a subservient, feminine roll."

Dane glanced back at her. She couldn't see his eyes but knew from experience that they were dark as oil and ticked.

Well, what she'd said had been true.

"Ah, he's just trying to protect you," Brad offered.

"From a wizard who can't even keep his mouth shut about the fact that he found a weakness spell? Please. I could take Donalbain with one hand."

Dane's voice came out terse over the airwaves. "No one said you had to come. You could have stayed home."

"This is my company, too."

"Now, now," Brad said nervously. "Let's not get into a fight. We're all friends here. Two of us are more than that. Y'all two need to remember that you love one another and Kumbaya and all that."

"Yeah, Kumbaya," Georgia muttered.

Don't get her wrong. Georgia loved her husband. But lately, with the start of their spell hunting company (they took on jobs for hire), it seemed like Dane was trying to push her more to an administrative roll.

"We have a daughter," he'd reminded Georgia when she'd given pushback about it. *"One of us needs to be around to take care of her."*

"These aren't hard jobs we're going on," Georgia had argued.

And they weren't. They were mostly the routine sort of thing, like finding a certain spell or keeping surveillance on a witch or wizard who was thought to be working with dark magic. Nothing too hard.

But it felt like whenever one of those types of jobs came up, Dane always took the challenge and sent her home to make dinner and pick up Judy from school.

That wasn't the partnership that Georgia wanted. She'd spent the past few years being a wallflower. Now she wanted to play. So she'd told Dane that she was coming on this hunt tonight no matter what.

He'd opened his sensuously gorgeous mouth to protest but had been smart enough to shut it just as quickly.

Back in the sewer, they reached the fork that Brad had told them about and turned. And stopped.

"Are you there?" Brad's voice crackled over the headset.

Dane released a low whistle. "We sure are."

They'd reached the end of the tunnel, or at least as far as they could go, because blocking the rest of the path was a table and shelves stocked high with colorful orbs—magenta, cyan, sunny yellow, the deepest green, oily black, and on and on the colors went, creating a kaleidoscope of hues from the lightest to those so dark they could barely be seen by the naked eye.

"Spells," Georgia mused. "Wow. What a collection."

Indeed it was—awe-inspiring and terrifying. Georgia quickly scanned the colors, reading them. There were spells that would make a person lose their hair, boil water, freeze air, unearth parts of the ground, give a person the strength of ten men, superspeed, X-ray vision —it was like you used all the spells and you'd become Superman, or woman.

What was Donalbain wanting these for? Not that it mattered, because they were about to clear them out.

Dane opened up a black bag, and Georgia followed suit. "Grab everything," he instructed. "Don't leave anything behind."

She quickly grabbed a small glass jar that housed an orb. "How long do you think he's been hording these?"

"To have this many? No telling. But he can't be trusted. That's been proven before. So grab them all."

They worked quickly, placing the glass as gently as possible in the bags. When they were done and every last spell had been taken, including the one they had come there for, the weakness spell, Georgia placed cushioning magic on the bag to keep any of the jars from breaking.

Dane spoke to Brad. "We've got them and we're heading out."

"Okay, just go back the way you came," Brad told them. "You remember?"

"We got it." Dane glanced back at Georgia and smiled. "You ready? Your bag's not too heavy, is it?"

She bit down a grunt as she hoisted the sack over her shoulder. "No, it's fine. I've got it."

If they hurried, she *would* have it. But her hands were already aching from clutching the bag shut and her back was bending under the weight.

Dane studied her. "You sure?"

"I'm sure."

She was not about to let her husband, who hadn't even wanted to bring her on this mission, to think she couldn't handle it.

Georgia could take whatever he threw her way.

They'd walked about three steps when Brad's voice cracked in her ear. "Um, y'all?"

"Yep?" Dane asked.

"I hate to say this, but you've got company."

Dane grabbed Georgia's hand as they rounded a turn. There, standing in shadows, somehow with an eerie blue light behind him (where had that come from?), stood Donalbain.

He opened his palms. Golden flames jumped atop them. "Well, well, well, who wants to play?"

CHAPTER 2

Georgia had never considered Donalbain to be much of a threat. That was, until now. He was a small man with wiry, dark hair that haloed his head, and his face was well-worn, suggesting he had drunk too much Jack Daniels and smoked too many cigarettes during his life.

But there was a scary energy to him, as if Donalbain was three seconds away from coming unhinged.

Georgia didn't like it.

"Stay behind me," Dane whispered.

She did not. If her husband was going to face off against a fierce wizard, he wasn't going to do it alone.

"Though I've never truly seen your faces, from the energy you're projecting, I recognize both of you," Donalbain sneered, referencing the fact that spell hunters usually wore disguises. "What were your names again? Oh, I believe we have a Georgia and a Dane."

Dane's jaw jumped. "How do you know our names?"

"Word travels fast in this town. How did you know I have spells down here?"

"Like you said, word travels fast in this town," Georgia mimicked.

"Touché," he replied. "Listen, as much as I'd love to stay and catch up on old times—"

"Do you mean ones where we had you hauled in front of the wizarding council?" she asked.

"Those would be them," he admitted. "But seeing has how I have no intention of ever going back there, why don't you hand over the spells that you've stolen and we can both be on our way?"

"You're in possession of some dangerous magic," Dane explained.

"Tsk, tsk. And I thought every child should be able to play with weakness potions. My mistake." He reached out one flaming hand, gesturing for the bag. "Now, I'll just be taking that."

"I don't think so." To Georgia, Dane said, "Step back."

Like she was going to do that. Georgia dropped her bag with a *thud* and coaxed Donalbain. "You want your spells? You're going to have to take them."

He glanced up and shook his head. "Why do spell hunters always have to make things difficult? Well, so be it, then. I haven't had the chance to practice my magical fighting skills in a while. I look forward to besting both of you."

Dane glanced over at Georgia before snapping his head back at Donalbain. The message, though silent, was clear: *Thank you for now forcing a fight. Remind me when we get home that you need a good talking-to.*

Or spanking. He could have been thinking about a spanking. But Georgia's idea of a little spanking didn't have anything to do with being reprimanded. Not at all.

"Come on, then," Donalbain challenged. "I want to see how long it will take for me to best two spell hunters at once."

What? Was he on steroids? Georgia wondered. There was no way that Donalbain, no matter how strong, could take on one witch and one wizard successfully.

Unless…

The flames in his hands went out, and in the near darkness Georgia heard a jar open and saw a flicker of blue light before it disappeared inside Donalbain's mouth.

Dane didn't wait one more second. He hit Donalbain with a line of magic. Power streamed into Donalbain, lighting up his face that was twisted in victory. The magic, Dane's magic, was supposed to have sent Donalbain falling to his knees or even flying backward, but it was not doing any of that.

Instead it looked like Donalbain was absorbing it.

Crap. They were in trouble now.

If Donalbain had absorbed the power, that meant he needed to release it.

"Run, Dane," she called.

But where to? Donalbain blocked the exit. Back, they'd have to go back and find another way out.

Before her husband could argue, Georgia yanked her sack from the ground and grabbed his collar, pulling him away just as a blast of magic, thick like a wall of flames, hit the tunnel behind them.

"He used an absorbing spell," Georgia said as they charged through the tunnel, away from Donalbain.

"You think?" her husband threw out.

"There's no need to be smart."

"Sorry. I'm just stressed." He clicked on his radio. "Brad, we need a way out of here. Like, fast."

"On it," Brad's voice said through static.

Donalbain's magic must've created interference in their communication systems. Hopefully they wouldn't lose Brad.

"Do you have a spell to counter what Donalbain's got?" Georgia asked.

"Thinking," Dane said.

From behind them, they heard Donalbain yell, "Coming for you! I can't wait to roast spell hunters."

For supper, Georgia thought. How did his sentence make any sense? No one was excited to roast spell hunters unless they were either cannibals or sickos. Perhaps Donalbain had become both in the time since Georgia had retired and then come out of said retirement.

Georgia glanced back and saw Donalbain shoot something from his hand. Colorful orbs scattered toward her.

She pushed Dane. "Faster!"

Where her feet had hit, the orbs landed, looking like sticky globs of colorful goo. They hit the sides of the tunnel, erupting like colorful pimples.

"Don't let them touch you," Dane shouted. "They're acidic."

"Now you tell me. Didn't you say that this would be easy? That Donalbain was nothing to worry about?"

"I hardly think this is the time to be arguing," he spat. To Brad he said, "We really need that exit. Things are heating up down here."

"Just one more minute," Brad said.

The minute seemed to stretch on forever as more and more balls of magic erupted around them. Donalbain was closing in, and he wouldn't miss for much longer.

"Hurry," Dane growled.

"Got it! At the next bend, turn left. Fifty feet in, there'll be a ladder. Take it up and you'll be at a manhole. That should bring you out not far from me. I'll be waiting."

"You'd better have some heavy artillery with you," Georgia screeched as an orb spewed its guts a few feet from her head. "We need reinforcements."

"We need time to think," Dane corrected.

Think? Reinforcements? They needed to be fast with both. Dane turned at the next intersection, and light darted from small holes in the manhole, illuminating the ladder for them.

Thank goodness, was what an exhausted Georgia thought. Her side hurt. Her legs ached from pushing them to their limits. Sweat fissured down her back into her panties, and it also pooled under her boobs.

She needed a shower yesterday.

Dane charged up the ladder and pushed on the manhole cover. "It's locked. Brad, it's locked."

"I'm coming!"

Brad was overweight and slow. Slow and overweight. There was no way he'd reach them before they had their Showcase Showdown with Donalbain.

Georgia took a mental inventory. She glanced up at Dane at the exact moment that he jumped down.

In unison they said, "Weakness spell."

Before they could open their sacks to search for it, Donalbain rounded the corner, golden globs of goo stuck to his hands.

"Well, well, well, look who's found a rat in a trap?"

"We have," Georgia said. "You've walked right into it."

He released a loud, luxurious laugh, one that Georgia wished she had the guts to lord over him. "I don't think so. You've both come so far. You nearly bested me. I suppose after this, I'll have to move my little stash, now, won't I? Otherwise I won't be able to keep my promise to Gator."

What in the world was a Gator? Or, who was Gator? And why would anyone call themselves Gator? That plain made no sense.

Dane stepped forward, blocking Georgia from Donalbain's attack. Donalbain's mouth made an O. "Wow. One spell hunter guarding another. You must have feelings for her. Am I right? This is going to be so much more dramatic when I take out spell-hunter lovers. I will go down in the history of evil as one of the great wizards of our time."

"Evil history?" I asked. "Is that really a thing? Like, are there high school courses on it?"

"College, actually," he informed her.

"Criminals go to college?" Dane said, surprised. "Will wonders never cease. You know, there should be a spell-hunter college. If there's a college where one learns how to be evil, then there should be one for the good guys."

"I agree," Georgia said. "We should start one. Or at least research this idea thoroughly."

"Do you think we could hire some evil professors to teach the classes?" Dane kept playing along as his hand snaked down into his bag. "You know, so that future spell hunters could really dissect the mind of our nemeses. *Nemeses? Is that a word?*"

"I don't think so."

"Stop it," Donalbain cried. "You're wasting time. Stalling."

"We're not stalling," Dane assured him.

They were definitely stalling.

The sticky orbs in Donalbain's (the wizard of evil, apparently) hands made his face look sickly. So when he grinned, it turned Georgia's stomach.

"It doesn't matter if you're stalling or not. I have the advantage. I've got two spell hunters with nowhere to go. There's no place to run, little hunters. I will kill you both, take back my spells and..."

"Will rule the world with your evilness?" Georgia guessed.

"Something like that. Now. Hand over the bags."

"I'm about there," Brad said in their ears. "Stand back."

Great. They just had to keep Donalbain monologuing for another minute and the tide would turn.

"That was a neat little trick you did," Georgia said, "sucking up Dane's power and then firing it against us. Where'd you come up with that?"

A proud smile lit up Donalbain's face. "It wasn't me. It was the Gator."

Dane shook his head. "This illusive Gator. All we know is a name. Tell me, does he have the head of one? Is that why you call him that?"

"You mock me," Donalbain said.

"Yes, I do."

"It's gonna blow," Brad said. "In three, two, o—"

A blinding flash exploded from above them. The ground trembled and quaked, sending Georgia flying onto the tunnel's ribs. Dane threw a jar at Donalbain's feet as he screamed from the explosion.

The glass shattered, and an orb hit Donalbain in the shins. "No," he screamed. "Not weakness!"

The goopy orbs dripped from his hands, their magic unravelling since Donalbain didn't have any strength to keep them going anymore. He fell to his knees, weeping.

"My beautiful magic, gone!" His fingers scraped over the tunnel's dirt-packed ground, scrambling to push the globs back together. But they seeped into the floor, disappearing from sight.

Dane pulled magical handcuffs from his belt and opened them. Donalbain didn't put up a fight as Georgia's husband secured them around the wizard's wrists and pulled him to his feet.

Brad's head popped into view. He smiled widely. "Whoa. You got him, huh? And we were only here for the spells."

Dane pushed the prisoner forward. "This is what I like to call an added bonus. Thanks for trying to kill us, Donalbain."

"Agreed. Definitely an added bonus." Brad's face turned to Georgia. "How're you holding up?"

She hoisted the sack over her shoulder. "Contrary to what my husband will tell you, I'm doing fine."

Dane's head jerked toward her. "She's just mad because I wanted to lead. If trouble was waiting for us, it was best if I faced it first."

She rolled her eyes even though no one could see since her night-vision goggles were still on. "Yeah, that's what it was, all right."

As Dane pushed Donalbain up the ladder, the wizard moaned. "Husband and wife? I've been bested by a husband and wife? What could be worse?"

"The wizarding council," Dane said smugly. "That's where you're going next."

Georgia followed him up the ladder and out into the night. "I'll tell you what I'm doing next."

"What's that?" Dane asked.

She pulled off her goggles and smiled. "I'm taking a shower."

CHAPTER 3

Headquarters for Spell Hunters Limited, Georgia and Dane's brand-spanking-new company, was at their house. That's right. The place where they made high-tech plans to infiltrate abandoned factories in search of villainous wizards was also the same place where they watched reruns of *Mountain Men*.

If that didn't prove Dane's age, then Georgia didn't know what did. What said midlife more than a man who gazed longingly at a landscape blanketed in snow and mountains, where the winters were harsh and the lifestyle, even harsher?

But anyway, it was the next morning and instead of watching television, Georgia was busy getting Judy off to school.

And it was not going well.

"I don't want to wear that, Mama," Judy exploded. "There's no pink in it."

Georgia lifted the blue romper that she'd ordered specifically because it went with Judy's skin coloring. "But it's so pretty."

"I only like pink and purple. I don't like blue."

Since when had Georgia missed that memo? "But it'll look so cute on you."

Judy folded her arms. "I do not want to look cute. I want to look awesome."

Ever since Judy had started school, she had developed a little personality that was much more independent than she'd been before. She wasn't exactly rebellious, just exerting her individuality, as Georgia liked to think of it.

And her individuality sometimes made Georgia want to pull her hair out.

Like right at that moment. Time was ticking away, and Georgia felt older by the minute. As if the permanent purple circles under her eyes were getting longer and would reach her chin any second.

"Okay," she said slowly, "what would you like to wear?"

Judy pulled open her drawer and rifled through the shirts until she came to a long-sleeved pink splattered tie-dye.

She held it proudly to her chest. "This. I like this."

It may have been the ugliest thing that Georgia had ever seen—a present from a friend at Judy's last birthday. Georgia had purposefully buried it deep down in the depths of the drawer so that it would never be found.

But somehow Judy had managed to resurrect the thing. And right now it was Dane's morning to take Judy to school, and they would need to leave soon.

"Fine. You can wear it."

"Yay," Judy squealed.

"Once you're dressed, come to the kitchen for breakfast. I've got it ready."

Georgia left Judy's bedroom and headed into the kitchen where Dane was making coffee. The back door opened, and Rose, their octogenarian secretary, shuffled in holding a box.

"Good morning," she said. "I've brought doughnuts." She placed the box on the counter and pressed a hand to the back of her hair to make sure her bun was still in place. "I thought after last night you could both use a few doughnuts."

Dane handed a cup of coffee to Georgia and gave her a quick smile before saying to Rose, "Oh, Brad already fill you in?"

"He called me first thing this morning to tell me." Rose waggled a finger at Dane. "You really need to get that man a life."

Dane chuckled. "He has one. I think he just likes talking to you."

"You must remind him of his mother," Georgia joked.

Rose swatted her away. "I don't want to be anyone's mother. All right. Then what are we doing today? What's on the agenda?"

"We've got a meeting with the wizard council at eight thirty."

"Oh?" Rose asked. "Are they coming here?"

"No, we're doing a Zoom meeting," Dane informed her.

"All that magic, and the wizards still want to use technology. What a surprise." Rose opened a cupboard and pulled out a few dessert plates. "Georgia, can I get you a doughnut?"

Georgia had worked out every day, had been eating only chicken and broccoli and in the past month she had still only managed to drop five pounds. Did she want a doughnut? Yes, she did very much. Would said doughnut put the weight back on her? Probably.

Georgia waved her hand. "I think I'll pass."

Rose's gaze flickered to Dane. "Would you like one?"

Dane's mouth curled into a warm smile. "I'll take a jelly-filled."

He could eat anything and keep his abs, his flat stomach. How did he do that?

Rose plated another for herself, and they sat at the table while Georgia pushed her hips against the counter and did everything she could to ignore her rumbling stomach. Even dropping her nose into her coffee and inhaling the rich scent didn't help.

Nothing could distract her from the doughnuts being eaten.

Judy entered the kitchen and threw up her arms, "I'm here!" All gazes turned to take in the precocious five-year-old in her pink tie-dye shirt and jeans. "What's for breakfast?"

"Eggs and strawberries with a side of toast," Georgia said, walking her plate to the table.

Judy spied the doughnuts. "Aw, I want a doughnut."

"No ma'am, not this morning," Georgia said in a voice full of warning. "Maybe later."

Hope filled Judy's voice. "After breakfast?"

"No, not then, either."

"Well, when can I have a doughnut?"

Georgia glanced at Dane for help. He was talking to Rose about something. "After dinner, for dessert."

Which Georgia knew she would regret. But a doughnut then was better than a doughnut now.

Judy's expression fell, but she climbed into her chair and started eating.

Dane finished his breakfast and turned to Georgia. "Hon, do you mind taking Judy this morning? I've got a few notes to go over before our meeting with the council. We need to fill them in on everything that happened last night."

After they'd securely tied up Donalbain, Dane had called on the council guards, who'd magically appeared within seconds and took the prisoner away. They'd done limited paperwork, but in order to make sure that Donalbain was correctly processed, Dane and Georgia needed to meet with the wizarding council this morning.

Since it had been the council who'd hired them in the first place, they would be killing a few birds with one stone. Georgia and Dane would brief them on what they'd found in Donalbain's lair (if one could call it that) and also finish up describing the attack by Donalbain.

But even with the meeting, didn't Georgia need to be preparing, too? The look on her face must've asked as much because Dane quickly added, "They sent over a detailed line-by-line document that I need to finish up before we chat. I would've done it earlier, but it just came through."

Georgia wanted to tell him that she would do it, but she hated paperwork so in some ways Dane was doing her a favor...by having her take Judy to school on his day.

"Sure," she said. "I'll take her. No problem."

"Great." Dane rose and stretched. "Rose. I could use your help."

Rose brushed crumbs from her mouth. "I will be happy to dictate your findings."

Georgia's mouth nearly dropped. Dane was going to dictate to Rose, and Rose would be the one filling in the report?

No, Spell Hunters Limited had not been in business very long. Rose had mainly helped Dane bring his files from his old job and organize them so that they had a database of criminals and spells that they'd found and where certain spells had been located.

Rose and Brad had helped with most of that while Georgia and Dane explained how everything should be organized. There had been some differences there with Dane wanting to do things one way and Georgia another, but in the end they'd managed to work it out.

The back door opened again. This time Brad entered. "Uncle Brad," Judy called, sliding from her chair and rushing over for a hug.

Brad wrapped her up in a great big embrace. "How's my favorite tie-dye-wearing kiddo? That shirt looks great on you. You should wear it more often."

"Please don't encourage it," Georgia murmured.

Brad laughed nervously, as was his go-to, before speaking to Dane. "Looks like we're all set to brief the council in a few. Have you finished filling out what they want?"

Dane shook his head. "No. Rose and I were just about to do that."

"I'll help."

Georgia's gaze snapped to the clock. Time for drop-off. "I'll be back in a few minutes," she said as everyone headed from the kitchen into the office.

But no one heard her. They were talking about what they would say to the wizarding council, leaving her all alone.

She smiled at Judy. "Ready for school?"

Judy nodded hard. "I'm ready."

"Okay, let's go."

~

IT SEEMED like the entire universe was against Georgia that morning because not only had she been basically booted from being in the pre-wizard council meeting that even Rose was privy to, but the traffic at the elementary school that morning was backed up to the road.

Like, really?

There was still plenty of time for Georgia to return to the house before the Zoom call, but she wanted to be able to prepare some, know what Dane was going to say. If the line kept moving at the snail's pace that it was, she wouldn't have more than a few moments to prep.

Her heart started pounding, and Georgia inhaled deeply until the beat calmed.

Her phone rang. It was Claudia, her sister. Georgia punched the button for Bluetooth. "Good morning, sunshine."

"Ugh. I don't think the sun is shining, is it?"

"It is, Aunt Claudia," Judy called out.

Claudia was usually a cup half-full sort of person. "What's wrong?"

"Nothing. I just have to visit the lady doctor today."

"Yuck," Georgia said, thinking of devices that did such things as opened orifices that should be left well enough alone, and slimy lubricant that seemed to stay on for days.

"Exactly," Claudia chimed. "But the yearly has to be done, so I'm getting it over with—top and bottom."

"Oh, it's mammogram time?"

"Unfortunately."

"Well, at least you get it all over with in one fell swoop."

Claudia yawned. "I guess so."

"Hey, I wanted to thank you again for watching Judy last night."

"No problem. What are big sisters for? Listen, I was wondering if you wanted to go shopping with me this afternoon."

Hmm. Perhaps a little retail therapy would make Georgia feel better. "Sure. Sounds great. I'll call you around eleven."

"Perfect. Bye, angel," she said to Judy.

"Bye," Judy said.

The phone call had distracted Georgia enough that by the time it ended, they had reached the point of drop-off. "All right, get your seat belt off."

Judy mashed the button, and the seat belt hummed back into its holder. She sat up and pulled on her backpack as Principal Brock opened the door.

He was a thin man with a warm smile that touched his eyes. He had a mop of brown hair with gray on the edges and wire-rimmed glasses that sat atop his crooked nose.

"Morning," he said pleasantly. "How about that line this morning?"

Georgia chuckled. "Yeah, it was quite an adventure. I almost felt like I was waiting to ride Splash Mountain."

He extended a hand for Judy to hold as she climbed out. "Oh, school is much more fun than any Disney ride."

"No, it's not," Judy chirped, which made laughter spout from both of them.

"Have a good day, Judy," Georgia called.

"Mrs. Nocturne," Principal Brock said.

"Yes?"

"I think Missy Hendricks could use your help with the PTO. Do you think you might have time to attend tonight's meeting?"

Ugh. The last thing that Georgia wanted to do was be beholden to the PTO, but since it was for the school, she felt obligated to help.

"I might be able to find the time."

"Great. Meeting's at seven. See you then."

He smiled and shut the door, leaving Georgia to wonder how exactly she was going to manage being a spell hunter and PTO mom.

Where there was a will, there was a way. And right now, the way home needed to be met quickly so she could make the meeting with the wizarding council.

CHAPTER 4

"Tell us what happened."

The head wizard on the council, Garryn, sat ringed by four other wizards, who wore their dark robes with the hoods down.

Georgia wondered who in the world woke up and put on a wizard robe? Weren't there other clothes that were much more practical? Like shorts and T-shirts, for instance? Robes like that had to be made of some very heavy material and were inevitably hot.

It was still the tag end of summer in Alabama—excruciatingly humid and simmering. There was no way Georgia would be caught dead in a robe.

Unless she was naked underneath, however.

Then the heavy material might be sufferable.

"Your intelligence was correct," Dane told Garryn. "Donalbain was housing the spell underneath the factory. He was housing a lot more than that, though. He had dozens of orbs, right, Georgia?"

"Right," she said, without missing a beat. "And when he attacked us, Donalbain had even more spells, ones that are more rare—sticky orbs that exploded acid and even an absorption spell. One that enabled him to draw magic worked against him and shoot it back at a target. I've not seen anything like that."

"Any idea where he got such power?" Garryn asked.

"He mentioned someone named Gator," Dane explained.

Garryn's brow wrinkled. He was perhaps in his early fifties with salt-and-pepper hair, a chiseled face and creases that fanned the sides of his eyes. Georgia had been out of the loop in terms of the wizarding council for a while, and according to Dane, the head councilman was somewhat of a newcomer but had made many great impressions, which was why he was in charge.

"Gator," Garryn repeated. "I'm not familiar with such a person. Is anyone else?"

His gaze swept to the other council members seated at the glossy conference room table. They shook their heads in unison, as if they'd woken up just that morning and practiced the move.

Garryn rapped his knuckles on the desk. Georgia noted that he wore a ring on the fourth finger of his right hand. An inky looking onyx was embedded in the setting. The jewelry resembled what a high school student would get for their class ring.

Garryn must have some affinity for his old alma mater, Georgia figured.

"Did you find out anything else about this Gator?" Garryn asked.

Dane's gaze swept to Georgia. Oh, that was right. Before they went to bed last night, she had promised Dane that she would look into it, but she'd completely forgotten what with having to drop Judy off at school and rushing to look presentable for the meeting.

She could feel Dane's laser-beamed stare on her. But without missing a beat, Georgia managed, "We're still looking into it. We'll get back to you."

Garryn gave a curt nod. "Sounds like a plan. Good work, all of you. Thanks to you, we now have a known criminal in custody, one who was certainly planning to wreak havoc on hundreds if not thousands of lives. Your testimony will help us come up with an appropriate sentence for him."

"It's worth noting," Georgia said, "that we don't know exactly what Donalbain's plans were for the spells."

Garryn's brow shot up. His lip curled slightly as if what she said amused him. "He was housing weakness spells and many others, as you said."

"Yes." Heat crawled up her neck. Sometimes she hated being the center of attention. "But he never admitted to any sort of scheme to take over the world. He had the spells and said he would have to move them now, otherwise he wouldn't be able to keep his promise to Gator."

The head councilman rubbed his chin. "I see. But does that mean you actually believe Donalbain was going to do something for the benefit of mankind with the magic in his possession?"

He had her there. "Well, no. Definitely not."

He smiled warmly. "Then I think we can safely say that our original belief about the situation still stands—that Donalbain was pursuing evil intentions and can be punished as such."

The council members nodded in agreement while Georgia's stomach twisted sourly. Maybe they were right. Perhaps they were connecting more dots with Donalbain than Georgia was. After all, she'd only thought of him as a petty criminal. He wasn't someone who possessed the kind of power that she'd seen him have last night.

Never before had he used orbs filled with acid or even been able to absorb magic thrown at him. Donalbain had changed. Why? How?

And he had planned to kill them. Wasn't that enough of a reason to throw away the key?

But something didn't sit right with Georgia. She just couldn't figure out what.

"And what of the spells you confiscated?" Garryn asked. "Where are they?"

The hinges of Dane's chair creaked as he leaned back. "We're housing them here in a special containment unit. We haven't had time to inventory all of them. Once that's done, we'll have them sent over for safekeeping."

"Good, good," Garryn said. "Very nicely done." He glanced to the other robed folks at the table. "If there are no other questions, I think we can end the meeting. Does anyone have anything else to ask?"

The other four shook their heads. Garryn smiled, the corners of his eyes crinkling. "Then I can adjourn this meeting. But we'll be seeing you soon—at the barbecue."

Barbecue? Georgia's gaze snapped to Dane. His face flushed. "Yep. We'll see you then." He disconnected the call. "That went well. Don't you think?"

"What barbecue was he talking about?"

Dane fiddled with the computer's keyboard, suddenly very interested in pulling up a website. "Oh, we're having one this weekend."

She crossed her arms. "We are?"

"I'm bringing potato salad," Rose declared happily. "And Brad's bringing the baked beans. He says he puts hamburger meat in them and broils bacon on top. Sounds yummy."

Georgia had tasted Brad's beans before, and yes, they were yummy. But even the temptation of good food would not cut away her frustration. "Why am I just finding out about it?"

"Oh?" Dane still fiddled with the computer. "Hadn't I mentioned it?"

"No, I don't believe you had."

He smiled widely. "We're having a barbecue this weekend. I've invited a few folks. It's just to help get the business a little bit of exposure. You know, meet potential new clients. The council is financing a lot of what we do, but working with private enterprises could be lucrative, too."

Brad laughed nervously. "Well, if y'all don't need anything more from me, I'm gonna go check my equipment and see what else has come in on the radar. Make sure that we're aware of all the bad guys we're supposed to know about."

Rose slapped her thigh. "And I'll help with the inventory. Dane? Georgia? Are you ready to get crackin'?"

Georgia didn't know what she was ready for, but it wasn't to do any cracking, that was for sure. But she didn't want to say that in front of Rose, so instead she just nodded and smiled.

"Sure. Let's take a look at those spells."

They spent nearly two hours inventorying every last spell and calling out the names to Rose, who marked them down. Rose had comments for most of them. Like when Georgia said that one of the spells was meant to make things grow, Rose managed to blurt out, "You mean, like a member of a certain male's body?"

Georgia nearly vomited up her breakfast. Rose was eighty, if not a day shy, and listening to her say things about a man's body was not exactly what she'd expected to hear coming from Rose's soft pink lips.

Dane, however, just chuckled and moved on. In the end, Georgia and Dane rattled off the names of nearly all the spells except for one that was amber with a gold center.

Georgia's gaze scanned the orb, but everything she saw didn't make much sense. "I've never seen this. Dane?"

He glanced up from the jar he was holding and placed it on the table. He walked over to where she worked and took the jar from her hands.

"It's strange. The color reads like a growing spell, like a vegetation growing one."

"Right, like the sort you'd put in your garden to make sure your tomatoes come in."

"Oh, I could use a tomato right now," Rose said. "That sounds delicious. I could sprinkle it on some cottage cheese with a dash of salt and pepper. I think that's what I'm going to have for lunch."

"Sounds good," Dane murmured absently. To Georgia he said, "But the golden center reminds me of a withering spell."

"Yeah, that's what I thought, too." This was why Georgia and Dane made such a good team. They were almost always on the same wavelength when it came to magic and spells. Not so much domestic stuff, obviously, but with their God-given talents of magical abilities, they were in sync.

"I'm very confused by it," Georgia said.

"I say we just mark it the way we read it and keep on," he told her. "We've still got more to go through. If the council asks about it, we can tell them."

"But I don't want to hand them a spell that we're not sure about," she told him. "We're the experts. If we don't know what it is, I don't think we should give it to them."

He smirked and the dimple in his cheek peeked into view. "You're right, as always. We'll hold it and I'll do some research, see if I can figure out what it is."

They worked for a few more minutes until they were done, and Rose declared that she was ready for her lunch. "You go on, Rose," Georgia told her. "Dane and I will clean up."

Rose stood and walked a few steps. "Now where is the door in this place? I can never find it."

After Georgia and Dane decided to work together, they realized that they needed a secret lair. It sounded all sort of superhero and silly to her, but in truth, there were dangerous spells that the two of them would need to keep locked away. So having an underground (basement) room where they could practice magic and even experiment made sense to them both.

So the couple had created a basement that extended down from the pantry in the kitchen. It was two rooms with lots of magic hidden behind fake bookshelves—an arsenal, if you wanted to know the truth—and lots of blue light to make it look like secret spaces always did in the movies—high-tech and fabulous.

That had been Georgia's idea, and Dane had gone along with it.

And the exit door—it disappeared after it was used because, well, magic! And so Rose was perpetually getting lost in it.

Dane rose and revealed it for her. Rose laughed at herself and exited up the stairs.

As soon as they were alone, Georgia struck. "Were you going to tell me about the barbecue? I mean, before the *day of*, that is?"

Dane raked his fingers through his wavy hair. "Of course I was going to. I just forgot."

She shot him a blistering look. He sighed and walked over, dropping his hands to her shoulders. "I was going to, but I just forgot. Georgia, I'm trying to make sure that we have money coming in, that I can provide for the three of us. Some things just slip my mind because—"

"Because there's a lot on it?"

He sighed and nodded. "Right."

She rose and he pulled her into a hug. The warmth of his hands on her back left imprints of heat. "Just don't forget—I'm in this, too. We're partners."

"I know." He placed his chin on top of her head and somehow managed to add, "I'll do better."

She pulled back and gazed up into his dark eyes. "Promise?"

His lips curled to one side. "Promise. And you know what? I can start by showing you right now." His fingers grazed the top button of her shirt, threading it through the hole. "In fact, I can prove it to you."

"But Rose?"

He hoisted her onto a table and nuzzled her neck. "Rose won't hear a thing. Trust me, she's old."

Georgia barked a laugh as Dane's mouth smothered hers in a kiss.

CHAPTER 5

"How'd the doctor's office go this morning?" Georgia asked Claudia as they both perused their favorite clothing boutique in town.

"Oh, you know; it went." Claudia rubbed the cotton of a shirt between her fingers. "This is so soft. Feel it."

Georgia stopped inspecting a pair of skinny jeans that she wished she could squeeze her booty into and felt the shirt. It was like rubbing her fingers over butter. "Oh, that is soft. You should buy it. It would look great on you."

Everything looked great on Claudia. Like, really. She was tall with sculpted legs and a butt that you could bounce a quarter off of. Even well into her forties Claudia had the body of an athlete. It made Georgia jealous. She wanted to wear skinny jeans and sleeveless tops without having to worry about the puckery skin under her arms grossing someone out.

But if she wanted to do that, then she'd have to exercise as hard as Claudia, and who had time for that? So those two things were simply not compatible. Plus, her knee was prone to twinge on occasion, usually right after she upped her workout regime.

Her body hated her. It was obvious.

"How're things going at home?" Claudia asked. "Now that you and

Dane are working together all the time?"

"Great. We love spending twenty-four-seven with each other. We can't get enough of it."

Claudia heard the sarcasm in her sister's voice and laughed. "So you're ready to kill him."

Georgia sighed. "No, not at all. It's just…sometimes I feel like a fourth wheel, what with Brad and Rose there."

"How can that be?" Claudia studied the soft shirt. "I'll try it on." She turned back to Georgia. "Why do you feel that way when you're one of the people in charge?"

"Well"—she dropped her voice so that none of the other shoppers could hear—"last night we went out to search for some…things."

Claudia winked. "Gotcha."

"And while we were searching, Dane insisted on going first and wouldn't let me lead."

"You mean walk headfirst into danger? He wouldn't let you do that? Is that what you mean? He wouldn't let you sacrifice yourself?"

Georgia scoffed. "That's not what I mean."

"That's what it sounds like to me." Claudia plucked the pair of skinny jeans from the rack and draped them over her arm. "Your husband is protecting you from a fate worse than death, and you're complaining about it."

"I guess"—she found a floral print top with a ruffle at the collar that would look cute with white pants. It might in fact be perfect for the barbecue—"what I mean is that, I can be the leader. I used to be."

"And now you're not. You're a housewife."

"Right. But I'm not really that anymore, either. I'm both—a career woman and a housewife."

"Which makes Dane a house dad."

"But it doesn't," Georgia explained. Or, at least she attempted to explain. "It was his turn to take Judy to school this morning, but because he had to prep for a Zoom call, he asked me to take her. And then he decided that we're having a barbecue this weekend and told everyone. *But me.* So it's like the rules don't apply to him. He still gets to be a career guy who happens to do his careering from home. But I'm still this housewife who on the side just happens to be someone who potentially stops dangerous situations from happening." She frowned, winding her way back through what she'd just said. "Does that make any sense at all?"

"Yep. Sounds like most things in life—the rules don't apply to men, but they do apply to women."

"That's exactly it!" She jabbed her finger at Claudia and realized that shoppers were peering at them through the racks of clothing. Georgia dropped her voice. "Why is that?"

"Because you're a woman," Claudia said with a shrug. "I don't know why that is, but it is. Have you talked to Dane about it?"

"Yes. No. Sort of. He said that he's trying to make sure that we're okay financially."

"I'm sure he is." She grabbed a V-neck T-shirt and held it to her chest. "What do you think of this one?"

"I like it."

It went over her arm to go to the fitting room. "I guess you may just have to wait this out, see how everything plays."

"Nothing will change if I do that."

"Then be supermom."

"If I do that, then nothing will *really* change. If Dane thinks that I can keep a house clean, fight bad guys and still have supper on the table, then he'll always expect that. So what do I do?"

Claudia's mouth curled into a smile. "I believe you've just answered your own question."

If Georgia continued to prove that she could do it all, then Dane would expect her to. But if he saw that she was better at being a spell hunter than he originally thought, a true partner—or even better than a true partner, a whiz kid—then that's where Dane would want her talents to be focused. He'd realize that was her strength and he wouldn't take her for granted by asking her to do his chores. In fact, Dane would probably leap at the chance to do his own chores. He might start taking Judy to school every morning just so that Georgia would have more time to spend being the brilliant spell hunter that she could be.

And if he saw that being a great spell hunter meant that maybe he might have to pitch in a little with the dishes, then so be it—he'd realize that was what he needed to do instead of lie down on the couch while she cleaned up after dinner.

Why was that, anyway? Like every mom Georgia knew had the same complaint—their husbands lay down on the couch directly after dinner. Was that some sort of secret ritual that all men did? Like, *dinner's over, let's synchronize our watches all over the Central Time Zone and hit the couch in three, two, one. Go!*

Whatever it was, it was a common occurrence in houses.

"What do you think?" Claudia asked.

"About what?"

A sneaky smile crept over her sister's face. "About your plan to retake your life?"

Georgia's stomach growled. "I think that I may need to iron out the details over lunch."

Claudia snaked her arm through Georgia's. "Well, what are we waiting for? Let's try on these clothes and grab something to eat."

Georgia smiled. "Sounds like the perfect plan."

THE ONLY HITCH in starting her otherwise perfect plan was that Georgia had a PTO meeting that evening. Which meant that after she got supper on the table, she would then need to race over to the school.

"Can you clean up dinner tonight?" Georgia asked Dane while chicken sizzled in the pan. "I've got a PTO meeting."

Dane balked. "Sure. Just tell me what to do and I'll do it."

Georgia stopped. Tell him what to do? Didn't he see her do it every night? Oh, that was right—couch time. No, Dane was not privy to the inner workings of the kitchen. "Um. Well, just wash the pans. Put everything in the dishwasher and wipe down the counters. That's important. Don't leave crumbs anywhere."

"I'll clean up." He gave her his crooked smile, the same one that had first snagged her eye all those years ago. "Anything for you."

He wrapped his hands around her waist and kissed her forehead. "You're only being so nice because you know I'm still mad at you about that barbecue," she murmured.

"Are you? I hadn't noticed."

"Right."

"But there are about twenty or so people coming so that means…food."

She groaned. "I've suddenly got to whip up side dishes for that many?"

"No, not just you." He kissed the tip of her nose, and it took everything Georgia had not to melt. She had to stay strong. "Rose and Brad are bringing things."

She barked a laugh. "I don't think one container of both potato salad and baked beans will get us very far. But don't worry, I'll come up with something."

"Great. Because it starts Saturday at six."

"I'll be there."

"I would hope so."

They stared at each other for a moment before the smell of burnt chicken filled the room. Georgia gasped and jerked away. "Dinner!"

"I'll help you save it," Dane said.

They did, in fact, save dinner. As soon as it was over, Georgia left for the meeting. She was a few minutes late and Missy Hendricks was already standing at the podium, waving her manicured hands around and informing everyone of why the book fair was so important.

"Because, like, it's reading, y'all," she said in a voice full of confidence. "And our children need to be good readers so that they can become good stewards of life."

Did Missy, with her blonde streaks and dark eye-lined eyes, actually know what being a good steward of life even meant?

Georgia peered around looking for an empty seat. Principal Brock caught her gaze and motioned to an open seat beside him. It was in the very back—perfect.

She sat and smiled at him. "Did I miss much?"

"Not at all. She was just getting started."

"Sorry I'm late," Georgia said.

"Don't worry about it." They listened to Missy for a moment before the principal leaned over. "I'm sure you've been busy what with your new spell-hunting company and all."

Georgia's eyes flared. Regular people didn't know about her gift. Which meant that Principal Brock wasn't regular.

He pressed a finger to his nose. "Don't worry. Your secret's safe with me."

She glanced around nervously before saying, "Does that mean

you're a…"

"My parents were," he explained. "But I didn't take it up. That life wasn't for me."

"So you can do…"

"A little." He lifted one hand and made a jazz-hand gesture. "I'm just a novice, really."

Well, would wonders never cease? Principal Brock was a bit of a wizard. Georgia had had no idea. Well, in her opinion it was always good to keep magical people close. They needed to stick together, after all.

"We're having a barbecue this weekend. Lots of folks like us will be there. Would you like to come?"

He pushed his glasses up his nose and smiled. "Why, I'd love that. I'll tell my wife. Can the girls come?"

"Of course. Bring your whole family. There may be lots of kids there. Even if there aren't, they can play with Judy."

"Great. Thank you." His eyes held a world of warmth. "I appreciate you thinking of us."

"Absolutely."

From the front, Missy's voice seemed to pierce the walls like a thousand spears. "Do I have any volunteers? Georgia Nocturne, I see you all the way in back. Would you like to volunteer?"

She had no idea what she was volunteering for, and knew that if she asked, it would be obvious that she hadn't been listening.

Though Georgia had a sinking feeling in her stomach that she would regret whatever it was that she was offering to do, she smiled brightly. "I would love to volunteer. Whatever you need me to do, Missy."

Missy clapped with glee. "Great. You'll be our very first person to dress up like Candy the Cat for the book fair! I'll be sure to have your costume ready for you on the day of the event. Thank you, Georgia. I knew you'd come through for us and the school."

Georgia's stomach dropped to the floor. Dress up like a book character? Oh, great. Maybe she should have asked what she was volunteering for before she signed up.

Well, live and learn.

Live and learn.

CHAPTER 6

The week before the barbecue was fairly quiet. Dane and Georgia spent most of their time in the house trying to figure out exactly who Gator was and if he or she was important.

It was also the beginning of Georgia's plan to prove that she was a better spell hunter than housewife. And the fact that she actually didn't have much to do in order to prove that plan did not help her.

She considered creating a crisis just so that she could jump into action before Dane, beat him to it and capture the criminal before him.

Then he would see her as an equal.

But as it was, they sat around the living room with their respective computers in their laps going through a database of criminals.

"Maybe Donalbain just said the name Gator so that we'd let him go," Georgia suggested, more as a joke than a serious statement. "When I last encountered that wizard, he was blaming everyone else for the fact that he'd just blown up a building by combining the wrong spells. He swore that it was because two rats were fighting that the jars got knocked over and crashed into each other, which caused the spells to mesh."

Dane chuckled. "Sounds like something he would do. But I don't know about Gator. None of the criminals in the database have his name as an alias. He must be new. Or"—he glanced at Georgia over the top of his computer—"you're right and he doesn't exist."

But something tickled the back of her mind on that one. "And that meant Donalbain was hoarding all those spells for himself?" She didn't buy it. "He probably was in contact with someone else. If only we could get it from him."

Dane shook his head. "There's no way. The wizard council has processed him at this point. They've locked him up. No visitors."

Well that settled that, then. "I guess we keep digging, see if we can uncover anything else. What about the spell?"

"What spell?" Dane asked innocently.

Georgia rolled her eyes. "You know, the spell that we can't figure out what it is, spell. Do you have any ideas? Done any experiments?"

"Oh, I have plenty of ideas." Dane looked at her through his thick eyelashes. "They just haven't gone anywhere."

She sighed in frustration. "What kind of spell hunters are we?"

"The cautious kind," her husband informed her. "I can't just go in and call on the magic of a spell that I'm not familiar with."

"The consequences could be deadly," she murmured. "I know, and you're right. But at the same time, we've gotten every other spell to the council."

"I know," he said under his breath. "But I just want more time with this one."

There was an edge to his voice that wasn't normally there. "Why?"

"Because I don't know what it is, and I don't want to hand it over without first being confident in that."

This was Georgia's chance to make good on her new plan. She closed her laptop. "Well, what are we waiting for? Let's see what that spell is all about."

The two of them headed into the underground secret room, the Batman room, Georgia liked to call it. The mass of spells had been cleared away except for the amber and gold one, which was perched on a table. Under the blue lights it glowed eerily as if it watched them.

That was ridiculous, Georgia thought. Spells couldn't see.

Dane pointed to it. "Every book of spells that I know of doesn't list this one."

"Have you checked the online databases?"

He nodded. "It was the first thing I did. There's still no mention of anything like this."

"Hmm. How hard do you think it would be to pluck off a bit of it and use it?"

His eyes widened. "You want to start sawing at it? When splitting an atom can cause a nuclear explosion, you think it's a good idea to hack off a bit of an unknown spell?"

She nodded. "It could destabilize it, I know."

"It could destroy the whole house with us in it." Dane's jaw flexed. "It's too risky."

Georgia tapped her foot in thought. Mixing spells could cause explosions. Slicing them up could do the same. How were they supposed to solve the mystery if they couldn't experiment on this one?

She snapped her fingers. "What if we copy it?"

Dane studied the spell warily, with one fist under his chin and his whole body bowed forward. "I don't know…"

"There's a copying spell in these books somewhere." Georgia, excited now, moved to their shelves of old spell books. "If we do that, and do it successfully, we can study the clones and still keep the original intact. It will let us know what exactly Donalbain—and Gator, whoever he or she is—wants from the orb." When Dane didn't say anything, she shot him a bright smile. "You won't use this spell and you won't slice it up, both for good reasons. I don't see any other choice."

He dropped his hands to his sides and straightened. "Your idea might either be the most brilliant I've ever heard or it's the craziest."

She winked and plucked a book from the shelf. "I'm voting on most brilliant. If copying is done right, you can make an exact replica. It's not done often, though, as it's hard and takes time. No one wants to wait around for the spell to cure."

He crossed to where she stood by the table and peered over her shoulder as she flipped the pages. "But I know it's in here. I'm surprised you didn't think of it."

He shrugged. "I was trying to find a way to keep the purity of the magic."

She narrowed her eyes. "This will keep the purity. It's just got to be done the right way. You're such a pessimist sometimes."

"I'm not a pessimist. I'm a realist. And as such, I know it's best not to tamper with a spell when I'm unsure of what it'll do. I have a family that I would like to keep safe."

She tipped her chin toward him. "Same here. That's why we're going to copy it and then experiment on it in the swamp."

His fingers traced up her arm. "Sometimes you say the sexiest things."

Georgia laughed. "Sometimes you turn unsexy moments into strangely sexy ones."

He hiked a shoulder. "Makes life more interesting."

She supposed it did, but Georgia forced herself to drag her gaze from Dane's thick lashes and hungry eyes to focus on the book. That spell was in there, she just knew it. All Georgia had to do was find it and they'd be on the right track.

"Aha, here it is. The spell for copying another spell."

She read the ingredients and Dane nodded. "We have all of that."

"We'll need to mix it and then pour a drop on the spell. If you want more than one copy, then we'll need to pour more than one drop."

Dane nodded. "Three. Three copies should be enough for me to be able to dissect at least some of what it'll do."

"And then it'll have to cure for up to a week."

"Fine by me. We've got the spell. Gator doesn't. So we should be good there."

"And what about the council? What will you tell them?"

"That I'm still working on it and if they try to take the spell from us, I'll inform them that it's much too volatile to be moved."

"Oh, going to tell them a white lie, are you?"

"Sometimes a white lie is what's in order." He rubbed his hands and tipped his head toward the book. "Okay. You ready to get this show on the road?"

She grinned widely. "Most definitely. Hand me the ingredients."

An hour later Georgia lifted a triangle-shaped beaker containing a deep blue liquid. "That is so pretty. It almost looks like Kool-Aid."

"Don't drink it or else it might clone you."

"Don't worry. I won't." She grabbed a medicine dropper from the table and pulled up a small amount of liquid. "Let's hope this works."

Dane unscrewed the cap on the jar. Working quickly so that the unknown spell wouldn't escape like a trapped lightning bug, Georgia squeezed a drop on top of the orb. The orb bounced around as if trying to shake off the spell before coming back to a slow bob. She then squeezed the second and third drops on it, and Dane secured the lid.

"We'll check it every day," he said. "When we've got our three, we'll separate them and take them to the swamp." He scratched the back of his head. "How will we know which are the copies?"

Good point. "I don't really remember. But if the copies are perfect replicas, there shouldn't be a difference."

He considered that before picking up the jar and putting it on a high shelf. "Let's just hope that if we wind up needing to make copies of a copy, that it won't work like trying to xerox a Xerox and lose its sharpness."

"That would mean the spell itself would change, become muffled."

"It could be catastrophic. Or, maybe good," he said. "It depends on the spell."

His theory sparked a memory. "Demona once told me of something like that," Georgia said.

Demona had been Georgia's old mentor before she'd turned on Georgia and gone over to the dark side, as it were.

"What happened?" Dane leaned his hips against the table, resting both hands on either side. "With the spell?"

It took a moment, but the memory sharpened. "I think it was a love spell."

He rolled his eyes. "It always is, isn't it?"

"Yeah." She laughed. "They're very popular, with men and women. It's not just women who want to catch the man of their dreams." She paused. "You're supposed to say, I've already caught the woman of my dreams."

Dane pursed his lips in thought. "Are you sure that's what I'm supposed to say?" he teased.

"One hundred percent."

"Well, it's true. I don't need a love potion. I've got you."

"Too late," she said, lightly punching his stupidly flat stomach. "Anyway, a witch was copying love potions and handing them out. But she was copying the copies and doing a shoddy job of it."

"Let me guess—it didn't turn out well."

"No. The men and women were giving them to their heart's desire, but the spells were so twisted that they didn't make people love them. It would have been simpler if they had perhaps lost one of their DNA threads and simply turned to hate."

Dane quirked a brow. "DNA threads?"

She waved him away. "Or whatever makes up spells. I don't know. I was just trying to make the story sensible."

"Well, not using DNA would have still worked."

"Whatever. Do you want to hear the rest of it?"

"Of course. So they didn't wind up hating the person who cast the spell?"

She shook her head because, according to Demona, what had occurred had been so much worse. If only those who'd been given the spell had wound up with hate in their hearts. That would have been a thousand times better than what did happen.

"Are you going to leave me in suspense?" he asked.

"Sorry. No. I got caught up in my thoughts. All the people who'd had the spell cast on them turned into monsters. Their forms became twisted and broken. All their humanity disappeared."

Dane's brows lifted in worry. "And were they able to be turned back?"

Georgia exhaled. "No. They weren't."

"What happened to them?"

"The council came in and…destroyed them. They didn't have a choice. And the witch was thrown into prison, of course."

"Of course." Dane glanced over at the spell. "I think that maybe I should put a colored ring around it, something that will just let us know which one it is. You know, in case the three spells we make don't wind up being enough. Don't worry, the ring won't be copied. It shouldn't touch the actual identity of the orb."

After relaying the story and actually recalling how dark the outcome had been, Georgia nodded. "I think that would be a fantastic idea."

CHAPTER 7

The day of the party finally arrived. Though Georgia had complained about trying to figure out the perfect side dishes to go with the meat that Dane planned to cook, she eventually settled on a light summer pasta dish, a tomato salad filled with cheese and olives, gazpacho and lots of grilled vegetables.

Rose and Brad could still bring their dishes. They would just be an added bonus.

Judy raced around the backyard wearing fairy wings because, you know, children, while Dane started heating up the grill and getting ready to throw meat on it.

Georgia had just finished up the last side when the doorbell rang. She answered and there stood Garryn, the head of the wizard council, holding a bottle of wine.

"Oh, if it isn't the lovely Georgia. Finally we get to meet in person."

Heat crawled up her cheeks as Garryn's gaze washed up and down, surveying her. He wasn't giving her a hungry look. No, that would have been incredibly inappropriate. Georgia had the sense that Garryn was studying her because she was a spell hunter, and working for him, nonetheless.

She had the feeling that he was judging whether or not she was up to par. And in her summer dress covered by her Minnie Mouse apron, Georgia felt more like a slug than a deadly witch.

She did her best to shove her feeling of inadequacy aside. "Garryn, so nice to finally meet you. Dane is in the back, and I'm just finishing up in here."

"Even spell hunters have to be moms," Garryn said.

Did he mean something by that? Georgia studied his expression, but Garryn just smiled as if he hadn't meant anything derogatory by it.

What was wrong with her? Georgia was so sensitive about her age and her station in life. She really needed to get over it if she was going to be any good at her job.

So she smiled and agreed with Garryn. "Yes, even spell hunters have to be wives and mothers."

"I'm sure you work twice as hard as most folks to do that."

That time, his words were obviously sincere. Georgia nodded and took the wine that he offered. "There is a lot to juggle." Obviously she didn't want him to think she couldn't handle being superwoman.

He punched his hands into his pockets. "My mother was a single mom. I know firsthand how hard it can be to raise children while having a job. In fact, she had two of them just to make ends meet."

Sadness stabbed Georgia's heart. "She obviously loved you very much."

He smiled. "She did. But anyway, I just wanted to let you know that though I may not have firsthand experience with what you're juggling, you always have an ally in me."

What comforting words. "Thank you. I have to admit it's hard to do it all, but I was a spell hunter once—"

"One of the best, from what I've read," Garryn said.

Her cheeks burned with embarrassment. "Well, I worked hard to become so. This company that Dane and I have started is almost a dream come true."

"If only there were two of you, huh?"

She laughed lightly. "Yes, pretty much. Come, let me take you to Dane."

As soon as she dropped Garryn off with Dane, the doorbell rang again. This time, it was Brad who had arrived. He had Rose in tow.

Rose handed her a Tupperware bowl. "Potato salad, as promised."

"Thank you."

"And I brought the beans," Brad said, chuckling. "Hope they don't give anyone the toots."

Georgia grimaced. "They'll be great. Come on."

Within half an hour everyone had arrived and they were all in the backyard, talking and drinking wine or beer. Georgia flitted around refilling drinks and taking empties, making sure that everyone always had a beverage. Principal Brock and his wife had shown up, bringing both of their daughters.

Judy and the girls were chasing each other on top of the wooden swing set that Dane had painstakingly hammered together over the course of a very sultry weekend the previous year.

Principal Brock pointed to the girls with his beer hand. "Looks like they're having fun."

Georgia smiled. "It does. I'm so glad y'all were able to come."

"We appreciate the invite," Lolly Brock said. She was tall with long blonde hair, copper skin and soft brown eyes.

Principal Brock, whose first name Georgia had discovered was Stan, placed an arm over his wife's shoulders. "We're delighted to meet people like us."

Georgia quirked a brow. "Like 'us'?"

Lolly winked. "Stan and I are both, um, magical."

"Oh, good. I'm glad that's what you meant and not something else."

"Something else like what?" Lolly asked, brows pinched.

"I don't know, but it could have been bad," Georgia joked.

Lolly and Stan both laughed. "But tell me," Lolly said, "you're different. I can tell."

"My husband and I are spell hunters. We search out spells that were created by the natives, for the most part. They exist around here in some of the forests and rural areas."

Lolly's brows shot to peaks. "Wow. That's so cool. And your husband does that, too?"

"He does." Georgia caught Dane's eye from across the patio. He lifted his beer and smiled. Georgia gave a little wave. "We work together."

Stan nodded, seeming impressed. "I'd heard of spell hunters, but I've never met one. At least not until y'all. I tell you, Lolly and I moved here last year and we were worried that there wouldn't be folks like us around."

"No need to worry about that." Georgia gestured toward the party. "Just about everyone here is like us."

Lolly shivered before shooting Stan a nervous glance. "I think what my husband is trying to say is that the last town we lived in, the job of principal he had before—well, um, there were some situations that occurred."

Worry fluttered over Stan's face. Georgia's heart tightened. "Situations?"

He dropped his gaze to his beer. "Yes, well, um, there was a kid being bullied. I saw it and before I could stop myself, I used magic to break up the fight."

"Like pull the kids apart?"

"Right," he confirmed. "One of the kids went home and told his parents what I'd done." He laughed bitterly. "They thought I was in league with the devil. Needless to say, I put in my resignation. That's why we came here."

"I'm so sorry."

He shook his head. "It's one of the dangers we face, isn't it? Being accused of something that we're not. The parents decided to believe the kid over me—which is fine. I shouldn't have used my magic anyway. It was just that…"

Lolly put a hand on her husband's shoulder. "He acted out of instinct and fear. He just wanted to stop another child from being harassed."

Georgia could understand that. She worried about her own daughter and bullies. The climate for little turd heads that were mean to other kids had changed since she was young. It seemed bullying was more prevalent than it used to be. Don't get her wrong. There had always been bullies—Georgia knew that. It just seemed that she heard more and more about it.

She smiled tenderly. "I'm sorry that happened to you, but I'm glad you're here. I think we all are. In fact, I like knowing that a wizard is at the school. I may be in the minority thinking this, but it makes me feel safer."

Stan smiled. "I'm glad you feel that way."

"I most certainly do. Now, please enjoy yourselves. Meet other folks who are just like us."

She moved away from Stan and Lolly and continued making her social rounds. She exchanged three empty beer bottles for full ones before making her way to Dane, who was talking to Brad.

"Brad," Georgia said, "I haven't had a chance to converse with you all day."

"Uh, hey, Georgia," he said with that nervous titter of his. "How's it going?"

"Any word on the Gator situation?"

Brad shook his head. "No, I was just telling Dane that I don't have any leads at all. I've been going through the databases by hand, 'cause I figured maybe our initial sweep missed something, and it's slow going, let me tell you. But I still don't have anything. But hopefully that'll change and I'll come up with something soon."

She hoped so. Garryn would want all the information they had on the Gator, which at the moment was absolutely nothing. Speaking of Garryn, where was he? Her gaze scanned the crowd, but she didn't see him.

"Where's Garryn?" she asked Dane.

"Probably inside using the bathroom."

She nodded absently. Now that she thought about it, she hadn't seen Garryn in a while—like several minutes. Maybe there was a line for the bathroom. Perhaps she should check and make sure that he was okay.

She excused herself and made her way to the back door just as Rose approached. "Georgia, I'm so glad that I found you."

"Hey Rose, is everything okay?"

Rose flicked her head, gesturing that she wanted a word alone. "Follow me."

Georgia followed a shuffling Rose to the side of the house, where no one stood, but from where they could watch the entire party.

"What's going on?" Georgia asked.

Rose peered over to make sure that no one was listening. "It's the potato salad."

"What about it?"

She grimaced. "I'm afraid that I may have made it this morning and left it out all day."

A slow fissure of worry wormed its way through Georgia. Okay. This might not be a big deal. It could be a small deal, in fact. Most things could be fixed. "When you say all day, what exactly do you mean?"

"I made it at six this morning."

And it was now six at night. Georgia groaned. "Why didn't you tell me this earlier?"

Tears pricked Rose's eyes. "I forgot. I'm older, Georgia. When you reach a certain age, you forget things."

"But you shouldn't forget that potato salad has to be refrigerated."

Potato salad, filled with mayonnaise and eggs, had to stay cold right up until serving or else the mayonnaise would go bad—not to mention the eggs. If left out to spoil, it could give someone a nasty case of food sickness, or poisoning if it had really turned.

"Okay, okay. How many people have eaten it?" Georgia asked.

Rose gulped. "I would say almost everyone."

"The kids?"

Rose shrugged. "Children tend not to like that type of food."

That could be their only saving grace. "Okay. I'll take the salad into the kitchen and throw it away."

"I'm sorry, Georgia. I really am."

Rose looked like she meant it. "It'll be fine," she said with a firm smile.

She hoped.

Not wanting to wait a moment longer, Georgia sprang into action, speed walking directly to the food table and grabbing the potato salad just as Claudia was going in to fill her plate with it.

"Are you stealing it for yourself?" Her sister said it as a joke, but there was worry in Claudia's eyes that pinged in Georgia. "Want all the potato salad?"

She leaned over and whispered, "It might make you sick. Don't eat any of it." Claudia's mouth formed an O and Georgia nodded. "Trust me. This is for the best."

Before Claudia could say another word, Georgia headed inside with the bowl. She dumped it in the trash and set the container in the sink, filling it with hot, soapy water.

When that was done, she turned around and exhaled with relief.

How many people had eaten the salad? However many, she prayed they didn't get sick.

She was just about to return outside when a scuffling sound caught her attention. She moved toward the noise and quickly saw that the door that led to their secret basement was open.

"What the…?"

She raced down the stairs. When she reached the bottom, she saw a figure in their Batman room, back to her.

"Turn around," she commanded.

Garryn turned around slowly. In his hand was the jar with the unknown spell.

Georgia tightened her hands to fists. "Just what exactly are you doing here?"

CHAPTER 8

"Georgia, I'm sorry. The door was open, and I let myself in," Garryn explained, still holding onto the jar with the unknown spell in it.

"We don't leave the door open," she told him.

Garryn shrugged as if that small bit of information was neither here nor there. "So what is this?"

Georgia stormed over and snatched the glass jar from his hands. "We don't know and are trying to figure it out."

His brow quirked. "Did it come from the raid on Donalbain?"

"Yes," she hissed. "It did."

Garryn scrubbed a hand down his cheek. "So shouldn't it be in the hands of the wizard council?"

He had her there. Georgia sighed. "We don't feel comfortable handing over a spell that we're unfamiliar with. So we're trying to solve that puzzle. But it takes time. As soon as Dane and I are one hundred percent certain that we know exactly what the spell is, we'll hand it over."

He beamed. "You like being thorough, huh?"

"You could say that."

"Well, I like a team that takes pride in their work. I'm sure you'll hand over the spell as quickly as you can. After all, you were just sent in to find the weakness spell."

"Which we did and gave to your office," she reminded him.

"I know." He lifted his hands in a surrender gesture. "You got me there. Look, I appreciate everything you've done. If y'all feel the need to keep this, then so be it. You won't hear a complaint from me."

That made her feel better. He wasn't going to demand they turn the spell in immediately. Garryn was actually going to give them space, let them do their jobs, instead of lording over them and constantly reminding them that he was head of the wizarding council and they were just peons.

Her rigid shoulders softened. "Thank you. I appreciate you being so generous."

He patted her arm. "Not at all. We're a team, right?"

"Right."

She placed the spell back on the shelf. "Now. I think it's time we return to the party."

Garryn gestured forward. "Ladies first."

She did go first, but made sure that she was the one who closed and locked the door behind them. Dane never would've left the door open. Neither would she.

So how did Garryn actually get in?

The thought tickled her mind for only a minute before she heard the first retching.

She rushed outside, behind Garryn, to see one of the guests holding his stomach and racing for the bushes. She heard the first splash of puke hit the ground before her stomach churned.

That moment seemed to set off a chain of events. Suddenly half the guests were running to the bushes and puking. Georgia's hopes that the potato salad wouldn't make anyone sick sank.

Dane crossed to her, brow furrowed. "What's going on?"

"The potato salad—Rose left it out and it went bad."

"The—" But Dane didn't get out another word before his cheeks puffed out and his skin paled.

Next thing she knew, he too, was in the bushes and more sounds of vomit splashing on grass could be heard.

Amid the chaos, Claudia rushed over. "What are you going to do?"

Georgia considered it before realizing something. "I may have just the spell to help. Stay here and make sure no one tries to leave."

Georgia rushed into her bathroom, where she kept her medicine, and pulled out a mason jar with a small green orb in it. "Don't fail me now."

She sprinted back outside, uncapped the spell and squished it between her hands. A green light splintered across the backyard, enveloping everyone in its path.

Her heart pounded. Her palms leaked sweat. Georgia stood in the backyard, silence surrounding her.

"Well?" she squeaked. "Is anyone feeling better?"

Turned out, they were. Georgia's magic did just the trick. All stomachs stopped being upset, for which she was very grateful.

Unfortunately that also meant the party was over. Everyone seemed understanding when Rose explained what she'd done. But they still jumped ship anyway.

Which was fine. It was getting late, and Georgia needed to clean up. Dane helped gather the garbage and close up the bag. They righted chairs, and Dane hoisted a sleeping Judy, who had curled up on one of the patio couches, into his arms and took her to bed.

When they were inside and Dane was helping finish the dishes, Georgia said, "I found Garryn in the basement."

Dane's brow quirked. "Why was he in there?"

"I don't know. He said that he found the door open."

Dane dried a serving bowl and set it on the counter. "I didn't leave it open."

"I didn't, either."

"Well somebody did."

She curled her hands into fists. "Are you suggesting that I left the door open and just forgot?"

"I haven't been down there since this morning, and I've passed by the door several times. I would've noticed if it was open."

"Me too."

Dane rested a hand on the counter and cocked his head. He was putting on his teasing expression. "Are you sure that you didn't open it? Go down there for something?"

"Dane, I leave it locked to keep Judy out of there. We both do."

He dropped his head and rubbed his neck. "If I didn't unlock it and you didn't, how'd he get down there?"

"That's the mystery. And he was holding *the spell*."

His gaze lifted. "The spell?"

"Mm hmm. The one and only."

"Why?"

"I don't know. I don't even know how he got down there to begin with."

Dane nodded. "I'll talk to him about it. Tomorrow."

"Thank you."

"But maybe the spell is a door unlocking spell and somehow it's magic trickled out—when we were copying it."

"Right," she said sarcastically. "I'm sure that's what happened."

Dane picked up his drying towel in one hand and a wet dish in the other. "Wife, are you suggesting that the head of the wizard council might be up to nefarious things?"

She shrugged. "If the shoe fits…"

He barked a laugh. "I have a hard time believing that Garryn is working for the bad guys and infiltrated our house. If that was the case, why didn't he take the spell to begin with? Why leave it?"

"Because if he'd taken it, he would've been outnumbered. In case you've forgotten, there were many, many witches and wizards at the party. Wizard council or no, Garryn would have found himself under attack."

"Good point."

"Thank you." She sighed and squeezed out her dishrag. "I don't know why he was down there. All I can say is that it gave me the creeps. Really, Dane. There was no reason for him to be poking around in our secret lair."

Dane wiped the last dish and tucked it into the cabinet. He turned to Georgia and took her wet, soapy hand. "You're right. Like I said, I'll talk to him. Find out what that was all about. Now"—he pulled her close and nuzzled his face in her neck—"I've still got some energy."

She pulled back. "Have you brushed your teeth?"

He rolled his eyes. "Yes. I don't taste like vomit, if that's what you're asking."

"It is."

He hooked a hand behind her back and pulled her forward for a kiss that tasted like peppermint. "See? All brushed."

"Even the back?"

"What is this? An interrogation? Yes, the back. Now, come here. Let's end this night with a bang."

She smiled as she sank into his arms. "Yes. Let's."

CHAPTER 9

The next workday, Rose showed up with doughnuts that weren't from her kitchen, she told everyone.

"I brought Krispy Kreme," she said, holding the box for Georgia to take. "It's the least I could do after the party."

"Thank you." Georgia took the box, and Rose shuffled behind her inside. "But all that's water under the bridge."

"More like vomit," Brad joked. Georgia shot him a scathing look. Brad nervously hit his fist into his open palm. "Too soon?"

"Too soon," Dane and Georgia said in unison.

They settled into the office for the morning debriefing. Brad hit a button on his computer screen, and an image appeared on the wall. "Over the last day we've received some intel suggesting that there are more spells like the two-toned one y'all found, located in the surrounding area."

Georgia gave a quick glance to Dane. This news surprised her. Dane, his chin on his knuckles, surveyed Brad steadily.

He knew! Her husband had known this and hadn't told her. What the heck?

"Where'd the intel come from?" Georgia asked.

"Other wizards."

"You mean ones from the party?"

Brad nodded. "Hey, you gotta use all the resources you can."

"Okay, so we think there are other spells like this one. Great." To Dane she said, "We should head out."

Dane shook his head. "The nuance of the color tone will make it hard to see in the daylight. We'll need to go around dusk."

"I can call Claudia and see if she'll watch Judy."

"No, Brad and I can handle it," he told her.

A jolt of anger rushed through Georgia. "But…this is our case. We're working on this together."

Dane's face wrinkled with guilt. "This should be quick and easy. Brad and I can handle it."

"But I want to be there."

Rose and Brad exchanged a look. Georgia was bringing a spousal fight into their business, but she didn't care. She was more than a housewife. Dane knew that. Why was he being difficult?

He gave her a pitying smile. "Next time. This time, let me and Brad go. You never know. It might not wind up being anything substantial, and then you would've wasted your time going out at all."

"Right," she said numbly. "Wasted my time."

Dane locked gazes with her for a few seconds before turning back to Brad. "All right. Next order of business. What've you got?"

By lunch Brad and Rose were gone, each having disappeared to their own houses to finish up some work. Georgia made herself a tuna fish sandwich and sat down to eat.

Dane entered the kitchen, spotted her and said, "Tuna, my favorite. Is there more?"

"No. I ate it all. The entire can. It's gone."

He paused, standing and staring at her. Then he gave a nod of understanding. "You're mad about the spell hunting tonight."

"No, I'm not mad. Why would I be mad? This is just our company. Did you hear that word? *Our?* Last I checked that meant you and me."

"It does."

She dropped her head and stared at the chunks of tuna that sat like gray bricks on her plate. "Then why do I feel like what you do is more important than what I do? Why is that?"

"I'm not trying to."

"You're not *not* trying to, either."

He shook his head. "That makes no sense. Look, if you want me to call Brad and tell him not to come tonight, that's fine. I'll do it."

"No, I don't want you to call Brad. That's not the point."

"Then what is?"

She rose and picked up her plate, holding the porcelain so tightly Georgia felt that she might crush it between her fingers. "It's that I want you to want me to come."

He quirked a brow. "I do want you to come."

"No, you don't." She swept by him and slid the plate into the sink. "If you had wanted me to come, then you would have asked me to begin with."

"It's a boring reconnaissance mission. It's not any action. You came with me to Donalbain."

She gripped the counter and hunched up her shoulders to her ears. "There it is. I went *with you*. You lead this company. You lead this house. I'm just your wife and the mother of your child who happens to also be a spell hunter."

Shock rocked Dane's face. "I've never said that."

"You don't have to say it. That's how you act. Whenever your plans change and you can't keep your regular day to pick up Judy, you have no problem getting me to do it. Because hey, I'm her mother anyway."

"You *are* her mother."

"That's not the point."

"Then what is?"

She exhaled deeply, trying to get her jumbled thoughts in order because they were a mess. She wanted Dane to see things from her perspective. But shouting at him and throwing a hissy fit would not do that. If Georgia was going to get anywhere with this conversation, she had to stay calm and levelheaded.

It was really too bad that her hormones were out of whack and that her hot flashes were coming more regularly. Not to mention her thinning hair. Jeez, she could see halfway to the crown of her head when she looked in the mirror. Okay, maybe her hair wasn't thinning that badly, but it was thinning all the same.

She inhaled deeply and turned to Dane. The look of confusion on his face made her heart ache. He really had no idea that he had been hurting her feelings, forcing her into a corner.

"I want us to be a team and we are. We have laid out certain ground rules that we hoped would help us keep things going smoothly in our lives, right?"

He nodded. "Right."

"When you ask me to pick up Judy for you, I don't do the same. I keep to my schedule because that's what we agreed on and I make sure that my work gets done so that I can do that. But when you ask me to pick her up for you, it's like you don't respect my time. You don't offer to switch with me, you just ask me to take on your role."

"I'm sorry."

She held up her hand, silencing him. "And when you said that you and Brad would go hunting tonight, I get it—you have history with Brad. We do have a daughter that needs to be taken care of, but I'm your partner in life and business. I'm supposed to be helping you find spells, track down bad guys. We're in this together."

Dane scratched his chin as if contemplating his next move. Then he stepped forward and slid his hands to her waist, resting them atop her hip bones.

"I didn't realize you felt this way."

"How could you not when I asked to come today?"

He cocked back his head and gave her a crooked smile. "I mean, I didn't realize that you think this means I don't respect your abilities. Trust me, I respect them. A lot. None of this means that I value you any less."

"Then what does it mean?"

"It means..." He shrugged. "I don't know."

"You have to do better than that."

He sighed and dropped his hands from her side. "I guess I'm not used to having my wife be in danger with me. That I'm responsible for your life when we're out in the field."

"You're not—"

"Yes," he said sharply. "I am."

Georgia searched his gaze, seeing only worry. That was when the lightbulb snapped on in her head. This was about Dane's manhood thing. His inner lion protector was being triggered every time Georgia was potentially put into danger.

"I've trained for this sort of thing," she said, trying to soothe him.

"I know." He rocked back on his heels and slid his fingers over her hands, picking them up as if using her to steady him. "But just because you've trained, that doesn't mean I'm ready for this. Don't get me wrong," he added quickly. "I love that we have this company. I love what we're doing. I want to work with you every morning and let you see this part of my life and I see your life. I love all of that. But as a man, as your husband, there are duties, promises that I made to myself when we married. One of those was to protect my family. That's my role. I'm the protector. What if something goes wrong in this reconnaissance mission tonight? I don't expect it to. Of course not. But what if it does and I could have saved you by keeping you at home? I guess…if there are times when a call only requires me, then I'm going to take it. It's one way that I can keep you safe." He released her hand and scratched his eyebrow. "I know that I can't always do that, no matter how much I want to, but if I can make sure you're secure and keep you with Judy, then I will. I realize that any big missions I don't let you come on means you're going to punch me in the groin."

"That is correct," Georgia said.

Dane laughed. "See? I can't keep you away from the Donalbain's in the world. But if I can keep you at home sometimes, that at least makes me feel better."

Georgia studied him. Dane was telling the truth, there was no doubt about that, but there still had to be an agreement between them. They had to meet in the middle if this was going to work.

"I'm sorry about the other day and Judy," he admitted. "I'll try to do better. I didn't realize you were so anal about your days."

She sniffed. "I'm a very busy person. Sometimes I like to read in the short snippet of time I have in the afternoon before you bring her home and she assaults me with details of her day."

He chuckled. "I get it. Okay. Yes. I'll do better. And there's one thing that I ask from you."

She tipped her head up as Dane stepped into her, taking his face in her hands. "What's that?"

"Patience with me."

A slow smile curled on her face. "I can do that."

"Great. Now go pick up Judy." He flinched when she swatted him. His mouth cracked into a wide smile. "I'm kidding. I'm joking."

"You'd better be."

He pulled her into a hug and murmured in her hair, "Of course I'm kidding. I love you. I'll do better."

"You will. Because you'll have me to remind you of it."

He barked a laugh. "I'd rather you than anyone else."

"Me too."

CHAPTER 10

Dane left later that evening to head out with Brad for the spells that were supposed to look like the amber and gold spell that they had in their basement.

Georgia kept herself busy making supper and eating with Judy and then playing a game of Old Maid with her. A game which Georgia hadn't thought much of when she was younger, but at her age, she realized the card game was terribly sexist. No one wanted the cranky old lady in their hand of cards. It was an obvious metaphor for life—don't become an old maid because you'll hate yourself and no man will ever come near you.

They'd be better off renaming it, *Keeping Your Virginity Until Marriage,* or something like that.

But anyway, after a game of the entirely too sexist and dated Old Maid, Judy took a bath and Georgia settled onto the couch with a glass of red wine.

That was when her phone pinged. It was a text from Claudia. *You still up? In the neighborhood and thought I'd stop by.*

In the neighborhood? Claudia never just popped in on a week night. Something was up.

I'm here drinking from boredom. Do you think that could cause problems in my regular life?

Claudia replied, *Only if your regular life is boring every day, which yours isn't. See you in a sec. Kisses.*

The doorbell rang a few minutes later. When Georgia answered it, Claudia swept past her. "Where's the wine?"

Her sister's hair, which was normally perfect, was poking out in places and she wore her pajamas. Georgia smelled a rat. She folded her arms. "You were in my neighborhood? Do you always go stalking at night?"

Claudia glanced down at her clothes and shook her head. "No. But I was just sitting on my couch and I was restless. I needed to get out and do something. Hence"—she pointed to her hair—"this."

Georgia smiled. "Come on. Let's get you a drink."

Claudia nodded and followed Georgia into the kitchen. After she poured another glass for her sister, the two women headed back into the living room and nestled on the couch.

"So, what's going on?" Georgia asked.

That was when Judy called to her mother that she was ready to get out of the bath. So Georgia excused herself to show Judy her clothes and brush her hair. Judy wanted to see Aunt Claudia, so she gave her hugs and kisses before Georgia pointed out that it was time for bed. After tucking Judy in and telling her a story, she went back to the living room and found that Claudia's glass was empty.

All she wanted to do was slump onto the couch, but Georgia said, "Need a refill?"

Claudia shook her head. "No, one is fine for me, thanks."

"Okay," Georgia said with a sigh of relief, "I think we're finally alone. What's going on? What's got you all worried? Are you seeing someone new?"

Claudia shook her head. Tears leaked from her eyes. Her lips trembled as she parted them to speak.

Alarm flared bright and hot in Georgia. She took her sister's hand. "Claud, what's wrong?"

Claudia took a tissue that Georgia handed her and dabbed her eyes. "You know that I went to the doctor."

Georgia's stomach tightened. "Right. You told me."

She nodded, keeping her gaze to the tissue, which she now twisted into pulp. "Well, everything looked great except for the mammogram. There was a spot. They're doing a biopsy."

"Oh, Claud." She wrapped her arms around her sister. "When?"

"They're calling me this week with the day."

"I'll go with you. Whatever this is, we'll fight it."

Claudia nodded. "I know we will. It's just that…"

It was just that there was a history of breast cancer in the family. Their grandmother had lived through it; so had an aunt and even a great-aunt. Claudia and Georgia were both high-risk, they knew that. Their mother had never been touched by the cancer, but that didn't mean it couldn't skip a generation and land on them.

"We'll get through this together," Georgia insisted.

Claudia nodded as more tears spilled down her face. "It's just that…"

"What?"

Claudia lifted her hands limply before letting them plop onto the couch. "I mean, what has my life been?"

"I'm not following."

"I don't have a husband. I don't have any children. I feel like if this is the end, then I've really done something wrong."

"Huh? You're the one who always said you didn't need a man to be happy."

Claudia nodded. "That's true. I don't. It's just that…I want someone to mourn me if I go!"

"What am I? Chopped liver? I will mourn you." Georgia scoffed. "Why are we even talking like this? We don't know anything about your condition. It might not be anything."

"I know, but I just can't help but think that I should have had kids, should have stayed married…maybe both times."

"To who? Trevor who cheated on you or Eric who gambled away your money?"

Her eyes brightened. "Eric was very pretty."

Georgia rolled her eyes. "Just because he was pretty didn't make him a good husband. Do I have to remind you that by the time you found out about all the debt he'd accrued; Eric had taken out a second mortgage on the house and your car was being repossessed."

"I really liked that Miata," she said regretfully. "It was a fun car to drive. Don't you think it's funny when you see old men driving around in them?"

"You mean old men around our age?"

"Yeah, but their hair's thinner, almost balding."

"But they're not in their sixties."

"No." She seemed to consider that. "No, I guess they're not. Oh God." Claudia started crying again. "I'm so old that when I see men my age, I think they're older than me. What has become of my life?"

Georgia took her shoulders. "Get a grip. You are having a biopsy. Whatever happens, we will get through this together. You don't need a cheating husband or a gambling one to survive. We're family. That's what matters most."

Claudia sniffled a few more times and took another tissue, pressing it to her lids. She inhaled several breaths that caught in her chest, but managed to exhale them out without leaking more tears.

Finally she gave Georgia a wobbly smile. "You're right. I'm sorry, just having a midlife crisis there for a second. I thought that everything was over. I needed to get a grip."

"Yes, you did," Georgia said flatly, which made Claudia laugh. "That's what I'm here for. To give you a grip."

Claudia pushed a bright smile to her face. "I feel better. Thank you, Sis. For everything."

Georgia smiled. "You're welcome. What else are sister's for?"

Claudia left a few minutes later. Georgia didn't want her sister to see her worry, but once she was gone, Georgia allowed herself to absorb what Claudia had said.

Possible cancer.

Her heart crashed to her gut. If she lost Claudia…Georgia shoved the thought aside. She was not going to lose her sister. Claudia was a fighter. She worked hard. She wouldn't just give up.

But was that right? What if all those little doubts that scoured her mind were digging fissures into her self-confidence? For goodness' sake, Claudia must've been down in the dumps to regret divorcing Eric and Trevor. Claudia had found Trevor in her bed, the hussy he was with underneath him. And Eric…Eric had lied to Claudia about their situation for a full year; meanwhile he'd been slowly selling and refinancing everything they had.

Like she'd pointed out to her sister, Eric had never told her that he was six months behind on payments on the Miata until Claudia literally saw the repo truck cranking the car onto its bed. When Claudia asked about it, the man hauling it away informed her that no ma'am, he didn't have the wrong vehicle. The car was being repossessed. If she had a problem with it, she needed to talk to the bank.

So Claudia did and that was when she learned their entire savings (half of which Claudia had contributed) was gone and that Eric was also four months behind on mortgage payments.

She knew he liked to stay up late gambling online, but surely he hadn't rolled the dice on all their savings over the Internet.

Turned out, he hadn't. Every time Eric went away on a business trip, he always swung by the local casino and threw down a fortune on the roulette table.

It took a crazy expensive lawyer and six months to get their affairs separated so that Claudia wouldn't have Eric's bad debt attached to her.

Funny thing was, not once had Claudia cried. She'd been way too angry to even think of shedding a tear. As far as she was concerned, Claudia had been hoodwinked. At least that was what she'd told Georgia.

Georgia believed her.

But now, with a possible cancer diagnosis staring at her, Claudia seemed to have forgotten how much pain both men had put her through.

Well if her sister needed some reminding, Georgia would be happy to make sure that she didn't forget—while she held her hand before *and* after the biopsy, that was.

She inhaled deeply and exhaled. Everything would turn out fine. It just would. It had to.

After tossing back the last swig of wine in her glass, Georgia rose and took the dishes into the kitchen to wash them. It was getting late. Dane should be back soon.

She picked her phone off the counter and texted him, but her husband didn't reply. Nibbling her bottom lip, Georgia flipped off lights and readied to settle under the covers of her bed with a good book.

That was when the back door crashed in.

Georgia leaped to her feet, her hands curled to fists in attack mode. She raced through the house and saw two figures.

She snapped on a light and gasped.

Brad held Dane, whose shirt was soaked in blood. She sucked air.

"Hurry," Brad said. "Dane took a hit. We need to heal him, fast."

CHAPTER 11

Georgia jumped into action. She raced into her bathroom and opened her cabinet. It was a mess—loose cords from hair dryers and curling irons lay like uncoiled snakes slithering over boxes filled with lotions that she hadn't used since goodness knows when. She shoved aside her TENS unit (she had forgotten that she even had one of those) and pulled out the mason jars located in the very back.

She used to keep a healing spell in her cabinet, but all she could find were useless—makeup enhancement, a spell that would make your boobs higher and flatten your stomach (she needed more than one of those) and one to remove facial hair.

Frustrated, she rushed back into the living room where Dane lay unconscious on the couch.

"What happened?" she asked as she ripped apart his shirt.

"He was ambushed," Brad said. "Out in the forest. One moment he was fine, talking to me over the headset, and the next—we'd lost communication. I left the van, and that's when I saw a big flash of light."

"Magic," she murmured. Dane's shirt peeled back to reveal a deep gash in his side. He moaned as she adjusted the shirt higher. "It's okay," Georgia soothed. "It'll be fine. I'm here. I'm going to take care of you."

But fear sank deep into her bones. How could she take care of Dane without a spell? That's how she'd helped everyone at the barbecue—with an orb, not her actual abilities. And now she was out of curative spells. Besides, curing a stomach ailment was very different than stemming the flow of blood from a deep gash.

Also, Georgia wasn't a healer. That was not her forte or even her specialty. The last time Georgia had attempted to heal someone with her raw talent, she'd been in high school. Claudia had fallen and bruised her knee. When Georgia tried to remove the bruise, Claudia wound up with a deep scratch that ran from her knee to her ankle. Blood had soaked through everything. Their mom ended up taking Claudia to the doctor for stitches.

But looking at Dane, there was no time for anything else. The blood had drained from his face, giving him a ghostly pallor. He had lost too much plasma. There was no other choice but to heal him.

She ran to the linen closet, grabbed a towel and thrust it into Brad's hands. "Whatever you do, don't stop applying pressure. Keep your hands on the wound."

"What are you going to do?"

She gritted her teeth. "Heal him."

Brad laughed nervously. "Did you find a spell?"

Georgia shook her head.

"Um, do you think healing him without a spell is a good idea?"

"Do you have a better one?" she snapped. "It'll take an ambulance at least fifteen minutes to arrive. You came here because this is closer than the nearest hospital. He doesn't have that much time. We've got to stop the bleeding now."

Brad's mouth set in a firm line. He gave a nod and did as she'd instructed. With him applying necessary pressure to the wound, Georgia rubbed her hands, warming up her magic.

At least warming it in her head. Rubbing her palms didn't actually do anything, but it made her feel better, as if she was supercharging the latent power that was locked deep within her core.

Georgia closed her eyes and breathed, honing her focus. She felt her power unfurl, rolling out like a velvet carpet before her.

"Don't fail me know," she murmured.

When they married, Georgia had locked her powers away because witches weren't supposed to marry mortals (Dane was good at keeping secrets and breaking rules). A few months ago, when she'd begged the goddess to return her powers, the goddess had granted her wish. But one side effect was that Georgia's power was bigger than she was. There was so much of it that it leaked from her. So she had to spend time blowing it off to keep her powers in check.

Now she had control of that magic but still didn't use it daily. Instead she relied on orb spells if she needed any help.

So when she called on her power, it rose up like a wave, nearly toppling her. It was a frazzled beast, one that Georgia had to squash down and temper.

She bunched her eyes shut tighter and reached out, harnessing the magic and willing it to plunge into her hands.

The power obeyed. She opened her eyes as magic pulsed from her. A golden river spilled from her hands over Dane's body. She imagined the gash in his side, the one seeping with blood, closing. She saw it being stitched up, pinching together with the help of her power.

Dane moaned and thrashed his head right and left. Sweat dotted his forehead, and his brows pinched together.

I'm hurting him, she thought. *I'm only making it worse.*

Georgia hesitated and started to lift her hands from his body. But even as she did so, she saw that blood still trickled from the wound.

She had to double down. "Move your hands away," she told Brad.

"But you said to—"

"I know what I said," she snapped. "Just do it."

He gulped but obeyed. Georgia pulled the towel away. The gash was as angry as ever. She pressed her bare hands to his flesh, applying pressure to stem the flow.

Then she closed her eyes and sank into her magic. She let her mind drift to the first time she ever saw Dane, how his crooked smile made her heart leap. Her mind drifted to their first date and how he'd brought her a single red rose when he picked her up. She recalled that first kiss, how he tasted of the mint ice cream they'd just shared. Their wedding day flashed through her mind—seeing him at the altar in his suit with his hair sprayed down so that it wouldn't fall into his eyes. The memory of when she told him that she was pregnant with Judy came to her. Dane had lifted her and twirled her around, only to quickly plant her back on the floor, worried that he'd hurt her. And she remembered holding a small squalling Judy and how Dane had kissed the top of her forehead and murmured that she was the bravest woman he knew.

Every good moment that Georgia could grab hold of flooded her mind. She focused on those, and the light spilling from her hands washed over Dane's body, making him glow.

"Please," she murmured as tears dripped from her eyes. "Please, work. I can't lose him."

And yes, their earlier argument seemed petty when she was faced with her husband's possible death. But as the golden light spilled off Dane and seemed to fill the room, his moans lessened. The blood seeping out from under her hands slowly became a trickle and then stopped.

The color returned to his face, though in all fairness, there was still a lot of golden light, so it was hard to know if that was what Georgia was seeing or an actual return of his golden pallor.

Even as she thought that, the light receded and slowly made its way back to Georgia, curling into her like a string from a pull toy.

When all the magic had found its way back into her body and the glow was gone, Brad exhaled. "Did it work?" he whispered.

She was afraid to look but had no choice. Georgia lifted her hands. Her mouth fell. The gash was gone! She had done it. Georgia had saved Dane.

He released another moan, this one lighter than the others, which she took to be a good sign. His lids fluttered open, and Dane's eyes focused on hers.

"Georgia?" He looked around. "What? Where?"

"Shh." She pressed a hand to his cheek. "Don't try to talk. You need to rest. But from what Brad's told me, you were ambushed when you searched for the spell tonight."

Dane's eyes flared with worry. "What?"

"He doesn't remember," Brad murmured. "It's the shock of it."

Dane shook his head. "I...don't."

"Let me get you a blanket. I'm not going to move you tonight, okay. Stay here, on the couch."

He glanced down. "Can I at least get out of these clothes? And I'd like to sleep in my bed." Before Georgia could argue, Dane was pushing himself up. He sat and took several breaths. "Dizzy."

"You lost a lot of blood. I healed your cut, but your body has to make more. I don't want you getting up and falling."

He nodded.

"I'll bring you a change of clothes."

Brad followed Georgia to the bedroom. "Do you think he'll be okay?"

"The magic worked. He'll be fine. He just needs to rest."

Brad leaned against the doorframe. "I feel bad leaving y'all alone."

She glanced up from pilfering through Dane's sleepwear drawer to meet Brad's gaze. That was when she noticed the deep lines in his forehead, the sweat that he was wiping away.

She might have almost lost a husband, but Brad almost lost a best friend. Never before had she done such a thing, but Georgia crossed to Brad and gave him a hug.

"He's gonna be fine. Don't you worry. If it weren't for you, he'd be dead."

Brad released her and sniffled. Then he laughed nervously. "Yeah, well. He's a fighter, that's for sure."

"He is."

Their gazes locked, and then Brad cleared his throat. "Listen, I'm gonna go. I'll call in the morning and check on him."

"Thank you, Brad."

"Hey, it's no problem, Georgia. What else are friends for?"

He said goodbye to Dane, and Georgia rounded up pajamas and a blanket. When she took them back to the living room, Dane was lying down.

"Think you can sit up and let me nurse you?"

He winked. "I think so."

They got him out of his black night mission clothes, which were more like army or militia fatigues than anything a person would wear out in public, and then Georgia brought him some water.

"Hungry?"

He shook his head. "No. The water's fine."

She helped him get the straw in his mouth. He took a few big gulps and sighed, falling back onto the pillows. "Do you remember what happened?" she asked.

His brow scrunched as he tried to pull the memory. "I was in the forest. Brad was talking in my ear about something. I don't remember what. Everything was going fine. There were a lot of spells—it's a good place to harvest. In fact, I'll take you back there."

She rolled her eyes. "Can you please stick to the story?"

He smiled weakly. "Can't even let me talk about going on a date without you grilling me?"

"You call spell hunting a date?"

He slid one arm behind his head and surveyed her. "Yeah. Don't you?" She shot him a scathing look, and he laughed slightly. "Anyway. The next thing I knew, Brad was saying that he'd detected someone nearby. He told me where they were."

"And you went to investigate."

"Because I figured it was the Gator."

"Of course," she said sarcastically. Leave it to her husband to nearly wind up dead due to his curiosity. But if it had been her, she would have done the same.

"Of course," he said. "I was approaching slowly and being quiet. I used a muffling spell to make sure of that. I thought that I had the advantage, and the next thing I knew, a bright light flashed and I was here, on the couch, and your face was shining above me like an angel's."

She cracked a smile. "But seriously. Did you get a look at him? See *his* face?"

Dane considered her question for a moment before he shook his head. "No, I didn't. I didn't see one thing."

CHAPTER 12

The next morning Dane felt much better, but Rose was all aflutter when she arrived. She dashed past Georgia, pressing a box of what smelled like cinnamon in her hands and rushed over to Dane, who was brewing a cup of coffee in the Keurig.

"Dane, I heard what happened. Are you okay? Are you feverish?" She placed the back of her hand to his forehead. "No. Thank heavens. Brad called me this morning and told me about last night."

Dane smiled feebly. "I'm okay, Rose. Thank you for your concern, but Georgia healed me right up last night. She's quite good at that sort of thing."

Rose glanced over at Georgia and smiled. "Thank goodness the both of you have magic."

"Yes." Georgia opened the box to find sticky sweet cinnamon rolls with chopped nuts sprinkled atop. "Wow. These look amazing. Someone must know how much my husband loves sweets."

Rose waved off the compliment. "It was the least I could do when I found out what happened. Since I'm not magical, I had to find some way to pitch in."

Dane spied the rolls and inhaled deeply. "Trust me. Pitching in like this is always welcome." He plucked one from the box and took a bite. A moan rumbled in his throat. "Oh, Rose. These are heaven."

"Glad you like them. Try one, Georgia."

She attempted to take a dainty bite, but the rolls were as large as her face. At the first nibble, flavors exploded in her mouth—cinnamon, sugar, yeast from the bread dough. One small bite wasn't enough. So Georgia bit off a huge hunk.

So did Dane.

Even Rose held the roll to her face.

"Knock, knock," Brad said, entering. He took one look at the three of them. "Whoa, are y'all like cinnamon roll cannibals?"

"Why?" Dane asked, his word muffled from his mouth being jammed with the confection.

"Because the three of y'all look like you're about to kill those rolls."

Dane handed him the box. "Try one."

"Oh, wow," Brad said after one bite. "I need more."

Once the four of them were finished stuffing their faces, they got down to work.

"First thing we need to discuss," Dane said when they were all situated in the office, "is last night."

"I should think so," Rose said with a sniff.

"What do you remember?" Brad asked.

Georgia watched her husband carefully, hoping that between the previous night and this morning he'd managed to remember something of significance.

But when Dane's mouth pinched into a grim line, Georgia knew the answer—he didn't remember a thing.

"Sorry, I can't recall who showed up. There was a bright light. That's it. But what I do know is that there weren't any of the spells that looked like the amber and gold one in the forest. If there were, he got them."

Georgia gritted her teeth. "You were ambushed. Somehow the information that you were going into the forest got out." Her gaze whipped to Brad. "Did you tell anyone what you were planning?"

He shook his head. "Absolutely not. This is highly classified. I'd never relay the information to anyone."

She looked at Rose, who stared at her like a deer in headlights. "What about you?"

"Dear me, no." She laughed. "Who would I tell? My Pekingese, Chi-Chi?"

Good point. Both Rose and Brad were loyal. They wouldn't have gone against them. The only other explanation was—

"We were tipped off by the attacker and followed," Dane declared. "Someone tailed us from the house to the forest and, in order to get me out of the picture, attacked. And the most likely person that could have been was—"

"Gator," Georgia said.

He nodded. "Exactly."

"And we know one person who happens to be familiar with the true identity of this Gator person."

"Donalbain," Georgia whispered.

"I think it's time we paid him a visit."

"Will the council let us see him?"

Dane's eyes darkened until they looked slick as oil. "Given what happened to me yesterday, I don't think they have another choice."

Brad nodded. "Rose and I will see what we can come up with on our end. See if we can maybe find a dusty corner of intel we haven't known about, one that leads us to the Gator."

"By Jove, we're on it," Rose concurred, swinging her arm in victory. "We'll track down this Gator and give him what for."

Georgia glanced at Dane. "You ready to call the council?"

His jaw twitched. "Readier than I'll ever be."

Garryn's face filled with concern. "You were attacked?"

Dane and Georgia nodded. They had requested an emergency conference call with the council and managed to get one.

Garryn ran his fingers through his salt-and-pepper hair. "And are you all right?"

Dane nodded. "I'm fine. A little sore, but thanks to Georgia, doing great."

"Glad to know." Garryn rapped his knuckles on the desk. "What can the council do for you?"

"We need to see Donalbain."

Garryn hedged. "This is most out of the ordinary."

"I know." Dane swiveled from side to side in his chair, giving an easygoing appearance. But Georgia noticed his clenched hands. Her husband wanted to pounce. "We've got to talk to him. He's the only person who knows anything about this Gator."

"You think he was the one who attacked you?"

"Yes."

Garryn's eyes narrowed. He didn't want to let them question Donalbain. Why? Georgia's thoughts flew back to finding Garryn in their secret Batman basement. Was he hiding something? Was the reason he didn't want them to talk to Donalbain because he was secretly Gator?

She shook the thought out of her head as quickly as it appeared. Of course he wasn't Gator. Garryn was fighting the good fight with them. He was on their side.

Garryn drummed his fingers. "Okay, I'll let you talk to Donalbain."

Georgia's heart leaped. This was great. "When can we do that?"

Garryn smiled. "How about right now?"

GEORGIA AND DANE were in a gray, sterile room. In front of them was an even grayer table and they sat in chairs the color of ash.

The air-conditioning kicked on, sending a cold chill sweeping across her shoulders.

She supposed the wizard council's jail looked like a human one—lack of color, morose, the sort of place that people didn't actually want to go and relax in. In fact, there was something quite unrelaxing about it. The bland hues, the frigid air, they put her on edge.

If the desired effect was to make everyone in the building uncomfortable, it worked.

Dane squeezed her hand. "You okay?"

She jolted, surprised by the warmth of his touch. "Yes. Fine. It's just this place gives me the creeps."

"You and me both." He scrubbed a hand over the stubble peppering his cheek. "The sooner we get this over with, the better."

She lowered her voice, unsure if they were being listened to. "Did you ever talk to Garryn about, you know, the basement?"

Dane brushed lint from his pants. "I did. Said the door was opened?"

"And?"

He shrugged. "Story closed. There's nothing else to it."

Before she could ask a follow-up question, the door opened and Donalbain entered, followed by a guard. The criminal's hair was askance, giving him the appearance of just rolling out of bed. When his gaze landed on Georgia and Dane, Donalbain's lips pulled back into a sneer. The guard settled him on the chair and locked the handcuffs onto a ring on the table.

The guard left. Donalbain leaned back in his chair and cocked his head. "To what do I owe this honor?"

Dane pressed his fingers together and eyed Donalbain. "Why do you think we're here?"

The thief laughed and scratched the rough skin on his chin. "I don't know. Is this a social visit? You wanted to see how I'm getting along in jail? You're hoping to vacation here next summer and wanted a first-hand report of what it's like?"

"Spare me," Georgia snapped. "You've got three meals a day and you're protected. No one's going to harm you in here."

Worry pulsed briefly in his eyes before disappearing. "I'm not concerned about being harmed."

Dane lifted a finger slightly, suggesting to Georgia that quite the opposite was true. "Of course you're not. But just because you aren't, that doesn't mean that I'm not worried."

Donalbain's brows shot to peaks. "Oh? Someone harm the dynamic duo?"

"Cute," Dane murmured. "It just so happens that last night I was attacked looking for more of that spell you have—the one with the two tones."

"Oh, the mystery spell."

"Do you know what it is?" Georgia asked.

"You figured it out yet?" Donalbain said, ignoring her question and practically salivating over his own.

Why was he so worked up about that spell, Georgia wondered.

Dane didn't answer his question. He deflected. "I think you might know who attacked me."

Donalbain laughed. "Me? Why would I know who did it?"

"Because you were collecting spells for Gator. You said so yourself. Tell me—who is this Gator and what do they want?"

He smirked. "Why should I?"

Dane's hands curled into fists. Instead of talking to Donalbain, he turned to Georgia. "Did you see the worried look on his face when you mentioned someone coming after him?"

"I did," Georgia replied lightly. "I wonder what that's all about."

"I think I know. He's playing a big game, pretending that nothing bothers him. But the truth is, he's bothered a lot. This jail offers protection, but if Gator knew that he'd lost all the spells, that we had them, I imagine he'd be pretty ticked off. He might come after Donalbain. After all, what does the two-colored spell do? If Donalbain started spewing out the truth, and even told us where to find Gator, his life would be forfeit."

Georgia clicked her tongue. "So we should definitely tell people that Donalbain gave us Gator's identity. That would be the best plan of action."

The whole time Donalbain's cheeks puffed out like angry red boils. He looked ready to blow his top. "Stop it! Don't do that! Gator will kill me! I know it! Don't say that. Please"—he broke out into sobs—"for the love of all that's good in the world, be kind to me."

Dane folded his arms over his flat stomach. "Then tell us everything that we want to know. Who is Gator?"

"I don't know, all right?" Sweat beaded on Donalbain's brow. "I have no idea who he is. He always kept himself covered up. But he asked me to find strange spells for him."

Georgia cocked a brow. "What do you mean by strange?"

"Spells that can be used as weapons."

Georgia and Dane exchanged a look. "What sort of weapons?" Dane asked.

"The kind that are arcane knowledge sort of spells."

"Dark magic," Georgia said with a gasp.

Donalbain nodded. "That's what I was searching for, for spells that were old and dark."

"And that's what you found," Dane said quietly.

"I…I think so."

"You *think* so? You mean you're not sure?"

Donalbain shook his head. "I never had a chance to actually use the spell, but Gator told me what to look for—a spell with the two colors.

Only the very old, most dangerous spells are made that way. All the new ones are different, one color. And you can combine colors to create new spells, hybrids. But not that one."

Dane was quiet for a moment before asking, "So. What does it do? This spell that Gator had you find?"

Donalbain shook his head. "I don't know. All I know is that I was supposed to deliver it. But that never happened. Obviously. But I can tell you one thing."

"What's that?" Georgia asked.

Donalbain's eyes darkened. "That spell is quite possibly the most dangerous magic that you've ever encountered. Using it is risky and could lead to one thing—both your deaths."

CHAPTER 13

"We have to see what those orbs are," Georgia told Dane when they got home. "See if they've cloned yet and if they have, take them outside and find out what happens."

"I agree."

They checked the orbs but found that their cloning sequence wasn't complete yet. They were still slowly splitting. Seeing the other orbs splicing from the first one reminded Georgia of Claudia and what her sister was going through.

"Dane," she said. "There's something I have to tell you."

She spent the next few minutes explaining about Claudia.

Dane listened quietly, nodding, and when she was finished, he wrapped her up in a hug. "It's all going to be okay," he told her.

She forced a smile. "I hope so. But I don't know."

"I do know," he said. "It's going to be okay."

"Yeah."

Just then her phone dinged, signaling a text. She glanced down. It was a reminder that Georgia was supposed to help out in the school library.

She groaned. "I promised that I'd do some stocking."

Dane nodded. "You go. I'll see what I can dig up here. See if I can go back and look at Donalbain's old partners in crime. See if any of them can somehow lead me to the Gator."

There were things about the Gator that Georgia considered. The first was she wondered if he knew that they had the orb. If so, it would make sense to her that the Gator would attempt to take it—if the orb was as powerful as Donalbain said it was.

"Do you think we need maybe booby traps around the house?"

Dane glanced up from his computer. "Booby traps?"

"You know, in case someone tries to steal the orb."

He smirked. "And just what kind of booby traps were you thinking?"

"Oh, I don't know, the kind where maybe a person winds up stepping on a whole bunch of steel balls and falls to the ground?"

"You're thinking *Home Alone*-style booby traps? I like it." Dane chuckled. "Tell you what, I won't set up anything quite like that, but I will create some that are similar. Just a bit more eloquent since I am a wizard."

"Sounds good to me." She shouldered her purse. "I'll be back in a bit."

When she arrived at the library, there was plenty of work to do. It appeared as if every book had been taken off the shelves and dumped on top of the carts for reshelving. She touched base with the librarian, Mrs. Roden, and then got to work.

For over an hour she worked her way up and down the aisles, quietly shelving books, when she came to a title that surprised her.

Arcane Orbs and Their Properties sat right between a book about Clifford the Big Red Dog and *Where the Red Fern Grows*. Georgia stared at the book, unsure if she was in fact seeing it correctly.

But when she glanced at the title again, it did indeed say the whole thing about magical orbs. Wow. Okay. Well clearly this wasn't a book for kids.

She peeled back the cover and saw that it had the initials SB inside. Stan Brock, surely. The principal must've brought the book to the library and forgot about it. That was it.

But what was Principal Brock doing with a book on arcane orbs? An uneasy feeling wormed through her belly. Georgia didn't like this one bit.

She leafed through the tome, which was just about as old as dust. The edge of the cover was frayed, and the inside pages were brittle. Turn the paper too quickly and it would disintegrate. As she read it, the book surprised her. There was a treasure trove of orbs mentioned and drawn, all describing ancient spells, the likes of which she'd never seen before. But the spell quietly multiplying in her basement was not one of them.

Why would Principal Brock have such a thing? One way to find out. Georgia told Mrs. Roden that she'd be back in a minute, and she stuffed the book in her purse.

She skirted children walking to the gym, smiling and waving at those that smiled and waved at her. When she reached the front office, she asked to see the principal, and a few minutes later Stan Brock came out of his office, all smiles.

"Mrs. Nocturne, to what do I owe the pleasure of your visit?"

"Can we talk in your office?"

His gaze shifted uncomfortably, but the principal smiled and nodded. "Yes, come in. Come right in." He closed the door behind her and Georgia sat. "I hope everything's okay with Judy."

"Yes, of course."

He took his place behind his desk and smoothed his tie before sitting. "Well then, what can I do for you?"

"I was in the library shelving books and came across this." She slid it from her purse. "I believe it belongs to you."

His face paled. "Yes. Where did you find it, you say?"

"In the library. It was with the books that needed to be reshelved."

He stared at it as if in disbelief that it could have possibly wound up there. "That's very strange. I don't remember taking it into that room."

"Well it wound up there. I'm not making this up."

He shook his head quickly. "No, of course not." His fingers twitched as if he was dying to have his book back, but Georgia still held it.

"My husband and I have recently become aware that there is a criminal searching for arcane orbs."

His eyes flared. "A criminal?"

"That's right. He's called the Gator. He had hired someone to search out spells for him, but we managed to capture that criminal and put him behind bars. But the Gator is still out there. Your book"—she rapped her fingers on it—"showcases a lot of the old magic. Spells to help you breath underwater, spells that create ice from fire."

"Spells that kill with one orb," he murmured.

Georgia's eyes flared. "I didn't see that spell."

"It's in there." Principal Brock shook his head. "That book never should have left my office. I don't know how it got into the library, but I'm grateful that you've returned it."

She didn't move to give it back over, and Brock smiled uncomfortably. He pushed his glasses up his nose and folded his hands on his desk.

"I suppose you'd like to know how I have that book."

"It did occur to me to be an important question."

"I inherited it. You see, the book came from my grandfather, Simius Brock. He was a wizard, one with great power. He spent years collecting orbs and researching what they did."

"To better humanity?" she asked.

"I wish." Principal Brock laughed nervously. "You see, my grandfather had what people call short man's complex."

Georgia was well aware of the complex. Short men tended to overcompensate for their small stature by being incredibly insecure and jerkish.

Often little dogs had the same issue, barking bigger and louder than other dogs.

But back to Simius. "He was a short man? I'm sorry, Principal, but I don't see how that's relevant."

"He was teased, bullied, like lots of short men. The short man syndrome became so bad in him that when he grew up, he was so insecure that he felt the need to make sure that people knew there was more to him than simply his stature. So he started searching for spells. He found many, as you can see. But he wasn't simply interested in searching for them; he wanted to know what the spells could do. He wanted to see how far he could push magic, what new power he could resurrect from its slumber."

Georgia suspected that she knew where this was going. "So he worked the spells that he found."

"He worked the magic on himself," he confirmed. "Most of what he discovered were benign spells, nothing that would make any big difference in a person. He could change ice to fire. But he wanted more, wanted to prove that he was more than simply a man of small stature."

Georgia waited for him to continue; when he didn't, she prodded him. "What did he discover?"

The principal picked up a green glass paperweight and palmed it, deep in thought. "First you have to understand what he did before you can know what he discovered. He cast on himself every spell that he could find that was old. He cast breathing underwater, mind reading, the gift of sight, and finally, he cast on himself the curse of mortality."

She'd never heard of that spell. "What did that do?"

"It gave him dominion over death," the principal explained. "He could see when someone was going to die. He could touch a person and know if death was near."

"That doesn't sound too bad. I mean, if he just knew that a person was going to die, then it's not all that horrible. I guess you shouldn't tell anyone that though. People don't generally want to know when they're going to pass away. It seems to me, at least."

He shook his head. "It wasn't just that. He eventually was able to touch and *bring* death."

A jolt of fear swept down Georgia's spine. "He was what?"

The principal nodded. "He warped the spells, turning them and churning them until they became something that they weren't to begin with. He morphed and hammered them like steel, sculpting them until they became more than what he'd originally planned. The spells—all of them—became something else. They spliced into his very DNA. Simius made it so that the spells would hold onto him and become a part of him. Yes, he beat the death spell into submission. He made it bend to his will until it did as he commanded and turned him into a walking grim reaper."

Her jaw dropped. "A walking grim reaper?"

"That's right. He teased out the DNA of the magic, cooking it down to its very essence and then joined it with his body."

It was an act against humanity and wizardry. It was one thing to work a death spell. Well, it was one *bad* thing, Georgia decided. Working that sort of magic was wrong, evil. It was quite another to take that magic and make it so that a person had almost unlimited power from a spell.

"Never in my life have I heard that someone could do that."

"Well, believe it." The principal dropped his gaze to the paperweight he still palmed. "The more Simius dug into the old magic, the more he discovered that there were spells that could fuse magic to a person. They're not well-known, but he found what he was looking for and made himself into a man that no one could ever push around again."

"What happened to him?"

"Well, he went after everyone who ever harmed him, hurting those who he said held him back. He went on a rampage. It took the entire wizard council to bring him in to justice. He had a family by then—my mother had been born. I can't imagine what it was like to see her father lose his mind, to become so entangled with magic and his own ego that he didn't care about his family anymore. All he cared about was himself and his own desires."

That was a bitter pill to swallow. Simius had turned against his entire family for his own warped desires. It sounded to Georgia like in his relentless pursuit of proving that he was worth something, he'd managed to lose his very soul, and his family.

It hurt her heart to even think about it. Even though Georgia and Dane were doing their best to find answers and stop bad guys, they always put family first. If something they did was in any way, shape or form likely to hurt Judy, they wouldn't do it. She was their sunshine, their reason for being.

"I'm so sorry about your grandfather," she told the principal.

He smiled warmly. "You can see why I need that book back. Like I said, I don't know how it got out of my office, but if I could have it, that would be great."

She slid it across the desk to him. "Of course. This doesn't need to get into the wrong hands."

"No, it doesn't." He took it and unlocked a drawer beside him, dropping the book inside and then locking it back.

And then she didn't know what made her tell him, but Georgia said, "We encountered an arcane spell."

His brows lifted, and Georgia explained what it looked like. He listened quietly as she told him that they'd worked a cloning spell but were still waiting for the multiplying to finish so that they could experiment with it.

"I've never heard of a spell like that. Just be careful," he told her. "Those old spells are powerful." The words were simple enough, but the look of worry on his face concerned her. Before she could ask if there was something wrong, Principal Brock rose. "I'll see you out."

A thought struck Georgia. "If your grandfather changed his DNA with the spell, does that mean that you…?"

His brow wrinkled with worry. "I'm sorry. I lied to you when I said that I didn't have much power. Yes, his magic passed down. The grim reaper gene expressed in me. I'm also one, just like he was."

CHAPTER 14

When Georgia got home that afternoon, Claudia called. "They're taking me in tomorrow morning," she told Georgia. "For the biopsy."

Georgia's heart hammered. "Okay. What time do I need to pick you up?"

"You don't have to come."

She scoffed. "Yes, I do. I'm sure they're not going to allow you to drive home alone."

"I'll be fine."

"No, you won't. Now. What time do you want me there?"

"Five is good."

"Then that's what time I'll be there."

She hung up the phone but couldn't stop the seeds of worry from infiltrating her mind. Claudia was concerned and rightly so. But Georgia didn't want her sister to know that she was worried, too. She had to be strong for Claudia. If her sister thought that she was concerned about the outcome of the biopsy, it would only make Claudia's worry worse. Georgia had to stay strong.

So she threw herself into cooking supper and helping Judy with her homework. Dane was researching when she put Judy to bed.

"Mama, what's wrong?" Judy asked when she was tucking her in.

Georgia shook her head. "Nothing's wrong."

She puffed out her lips and frowned. "I don't believe you."

Georgia laughed. "Big words from such a little girl."

Judy crossed her arms. "I'm a big girl."

"That's true. You are a big girl."

"What's wrong?" Judy asked again.

Georgia sighed. There was no point in hiding the truth from her daughter. "Tomorrow, Daddy's going to take you to school because I have to be with Aunt Claudia."

"Oh." She tapped her fingers in thought. "Why do you have to be with her?"

"She's going to the hospital for a test and she's scared."

"Why? Didn't she study?"

A smile spread across Georgia's face. "It's not that kind of test. There's no studying for it. It's different. They're checking to see if she's sick."

"Can't she just take her temperature and see if she's sick?"

Georgia brushed Judy's curls from her forehead. "It's not that type of sick, sweetheart. I wish it was, but this is a bit more complicated."

"Oh," she said, brow wrinkled.

"But don't you worry, everything's going to be okay." She pulled the covers up to Judy's chin. "Let's say a prayer for Aunt Claudia, okay?"

Judy nodded. "Okay."

Georgia said a prayer, and then she kissed Judy good night and went back downstairs. She said good night to Dane, who was still working, and then climbed into her own bed, saying another prayer for Claudia before drifting off to sleep.

The next morning she picked Claudia up promptly at five and headed over to the hospital. She sat with her in the bay while the nurses put in her IV and the anesthesia team came around and introduced themselves.

When the nurses had cleared the room, Claudia reached for Georgia, who took her hand. "I'm nervous," she confessed.

"Me too. But it's all going to be okay," Georgia said. "Whatever the outcome, we'll get through it together."

Claudia nodded. "Yes, we will."

A little while later they wheeled Claudia back and Georgia found a spot in the waiting room. Her mind was reeling and watching television wasn't doing anything for her. She'd brought her laptop in case she felt in the mood to do some work. Since the TV wasn't offering any sort of distraction, she fired up her computer and started surfing old wizard news clippings to see if any of them mentioned the word *Gator* or anything that resembled it.

After all, it was possible that the Gator was a new name for an old criminal. And after what Principal Brock had told her that it was possible to fuse spells to a wizard's or witch's DNA, she had a feeling the sooner they found this Gator, the better.

Her search didn't reveal anything at first. Most of the criminals were arrested for the usual stuff—love potions sold to humans, flying spells that went terribly wrong and ended up causing witches to fall to the ground while in midair. Luckily the witches hadn't been hurt. And on the articles went.

Georgia thought that she'd come to a dead end when a headline snagged her attention—CACHE OF ORBS LINKED TO SPECIAL PROSECUTOR.

"Cache of orbs?" she murmured. "What does that mean?"

She scanned the article, which was exactly as it described—about a prosecutor who wound up being caught with a cache of orbs that were stolen. The orbs themselves were supposed to have been given to the wizard council for safekeeping, but somehow they were never transferred and the prosecutor kept them for himself.

That sounded like bad practice to Georgia. The only reason she could figure the prosecutor wouldn't have turned in the magic was because he wanted to use it. That scenario didn't quite work out the way he'd planned though, because the magic was discovered in his possession. She snickered. Folks always thought that they can get away with things, that they were above the law. The truth was, they weren't. Sooner or later people's crimes caught up with them. This story was no different.

She kept reading the article, looking for the prosecutor's name, but it was as if the paper didn't want to give it up. Finally, when she reached the very bottom of the text, the story relinquished the special prosecutor's identity.

Georgia sucked air.

The man who had kept the orbs for himself was none other than Garryn.

Claudia was ready to go home a few hours later. After she read the article, Georgia had spent the rest of the morning silently freaking out, trying to figure out what to do.

Garryn, their fearless wizard council leader, was a criminal. Worse, he had a penchant for rare and interesting spells. He'd been on her radar ever since she'd discovered him snooping in their basement.

But if he'd wanted the two-tone spell, why didn't he take it? Easy. Because Georgia had discovered him in there. He couldn't exactly have a magical throwdown against them in the middle of the family barbecue, now could he? No. Garryn had to bide his time.

Which meant Georgia had time to get Dane up to speed on what she'd discovered.

Georgia took Claudia home and made sure that she had everything that she needed—comfy throw blanket, some warm soup, and a glass of iced tea beside her, and then Georgia left, promising to check on her sister later.

"When did they say the biopsy would be back?"

"In a couple of days," Claudia said.

Georgia smiled. "It's all going to work out. Whatever happens, we'll get through it together."

Claudia took her sister's hand. "I know. We will."

Georgia said goodbye and raced home. She found Dane in the basement. "Garryn is a criminal."

Dane glanced up from the bench he was working at. He studied his wife and said slowly, "You're out of breath. Did he just chase you here?"

If she'd had something in her hand, she would've tossed it at him. "No. Of course not. I just got back from dropping Claudia at home."

"How is she?"

"She's okay. We'll know the results in a few days." She crossed to him. "But while I was waiting for her, I went through some old newspaper reports and discovered that Garryn used to be a special prosecutor for the wizard council until he was found with his hand in the spell cookie jar."

Dane quirked a brow. "Is that so?"

"He stole spells, Dane. It's a big deal."

"It couldn't have been that big of a deal because they made him head of the wizard council."

She slapped her thigh in frustration. "He probably paid them off. I told you that I found him sneaking around in our basement. He was snooping."

Dane glanced around the room. "Did he take anything?"

"I don't...know. I don't think so." Before Dane could say that since Garryn hadn't taken anything, he wasn't bad, she added, "It was weird, Dane. Spooky and strange. I think we should investigate him."

Dane laughed. "You're kidding, right? You want to spy on the head of the wizard council?"

"That's right. That's exactly what I want to do."

He shook his head. "And how much trouble do you think we'd get into for doing that?"

"None when we're called heroes because we located Gator, who has been hiding under our noses."

"Or thrown into a looney bin for suggesting that Garryn is bad to begin with."

She shrugged. "There's something not right about him."

Dane gave her a long, hard look. "I know that you want to find Gator as much as I do. We don't know the wizard's plans and that freaks you out. It freaks me out, too. It worries me. Anyone who would pay a spell hunter to collect dangerous orbs is someone that we need to be worried about. I get that. I'm right there with you. But we can't simply decide that the head of the wizard council is the bad guy and get some sort of mob mentality about him. That's not right and you know it. We have no proof."

"Then let's get some."

His jaw twitched. "And how do you propose we do that?"

"I don't know. Maybe we spy on him."

"No. We're not doing that." She shook her head but Dane continued.

"You do that, you go and start digging into him and he finds out, it'll be the end of us. Our careers as spell hunters will be over. You know we can't accuse him without evidence. Yes, I think it's weird that he was found with a bunch of orbs, but I have to think there was a good reason for him to have then become head of the council. Don't you think so, too?"

No, she wanted to say. But instead of arguing, Georgia shrugged. "I don't know the reason. That's why I want to investigate it."

He pressed the heels of his hands to his eyes in frustration. "We were hired to go after Donalbain. We did that. We turned him in. We weren't hired to investigate anyone else. Yes, we're still trying to figure out who the Gator is, but I promise you right now that it isn't Garryn. It's not him. He's not a criminal mastermind that's managed to fool so many people."

She folded her arms. "And how do you know?"

He rolled his eyes. "Because I just do. Georgia"—he rose and crossed to her, taking his wife in his arms—"I'm on your side and am apt to believe most anything that you tell me. But this—I know for a fact isn't right. Garryn is not the bad guy here. He's on our side. No, I can't explain away his actions, but I don't have any sense that he's one of the bad guys. Trust me on this. Will you?"

She glanced up at Dane. His eyes were full of tenderness as his hands lightly stroked her shoulders. Georgia wanted to say yes. She wanted to tell him that of course she was on his side and believed him. Yes, it was silly of her to be suspicious of Garryn. After all, he'd given them absolutely no reason to question him. He had let them speak to Donalbain when they asked. If he was connected to Donalbain, he wouldn't have done that for fear of being discovered. Also, he hadn't given her a hard time about the fact that they had the amber and gold spell. He'd acted as their friend.

Perhaps Georgia *was* wrong and jumping to conclusions. Dane was more than likely right. She was barking up the wrong tree.

But even if that was true, why was she still having such a hard time accepting that Garryn was on their side? As she looked up at Dane, she knew that going against him at this time wouldn't be right. So she swallowed down her worry.

"Okay, I'll forget it."

Dane smiled. "Now, I have a surprise for you."

She quirked a brow. "What is it?"

Dane grabbed a mason jar from behind him. The two-toned orb cloning was complete. "What do you say about heading out tonight and playing with some magic?"

Georgia grinned. "Sounds like an awesome plan."

CHAPTER 15

Rose arrived later that night to watch Judy. She shuffled into the house carrying a basket on her arm. "I made some banana bread. I thought Judy might like that."

"Yes," Georgia said. "She'll love it. Thank you for coming at such short notice."

Rose scooted past her and waved her hand. "It's no trouble. I'm happy to help however I can."

"Thank you."

"Now," Rose said, depositing the basket on a table. "Get out of here. I'll take good care of Judy." She glanced around. "Speaking of, where is she?"

"Here I am," called the girl as she came into the kitchen holding a deck of cards. "Want to play Old Maid?"

"Of course I do." Rose opened her palm, and Judy dropped the stack into it. "You'll be lucky to beat me. I'm an Old Maid champion."

Judy's eyes widened. "Wow. A champion? I hope that I can beat you. If I can't, will you just go easy on me?"

Dane entered and smiled. "Judy's a bit competitive."

"So am I," Rose said with a twinkle in her eyes. "But I tell you what, I'll go easy on you. Come on."

They disappeared into the living room, and Dane and Georgia left.

The whole way over to the forest, Georgia's nerves were firing on all cylinders. The last time that Dane had gone out at night, he'd almost been killed. What if they were being followed? What if the same person who attacked Dane took them both by surprise?

She couldn't think like that. Georgia had to remain confident that they would be fine.

"I'm worried, too," Dane murmured, as if reading her mind. "We're going someplace we haven't been before, but I didn't tell anyone. It's an open field. No one can sneak up behind us."

"Oh, thank goodness," she said, relieved. "You don't know how happy that makes me to hear that."

His hands tightened on the steering wheel. "Trust me, I wasn't going to put us in unnecessary danger."

She smiled. "I always knew there was a reason why I loved you."

His brow arched. "Is that the only reason? Because I take precautions?"

"Maybe."

He chuckled. "Apparently I'm not doing my job right then."

She laughed with him. "I'd say that you're doing something right."

He glanced over, his eyes full of hunger. "I hope so."

"Okay, don't get that look on your face. We've got work to do."

They reached an abandoned field out in the middle of the country. Dane stopped the SUV. "Here we are. Let's see what these orbs can do." Dane had only brought the clones, having left the original orb back in the basement. He pulled the jar from the glove box and handed it to Georgia. "I'm putting you in charge."

"Great, because I have no plan on how to test out this magic."

He winked. "Lucky for you, I do."

"Well, I can't wait for you to show me."

They got out. The night was crisp and cool. Crickets chirped all around them, their songs impregnating the night. The field was last year's corn crop, or so it appeared to Georgia, with its matted brown stalks and bumpy earth.

Dane pulled a light orb from his pocket and released it. The magic hovered in the air around them, illuminating the night.

"In order to test these orbs, we have to try various experiments."

"Not on us, right?" Georgia said hopefully.

"Not on us," he confirmed. "We'll try the first few in the air, see if anything changes."

Dane pulled on a pair of gloves and took one of the orbs in his hands. Using a blade that he summoned from the air, he sliced a sliver of orb away from the whole and tossed it into the air.

If it was a spell that became activated by the atmosphere, it would shimmer and change. For instance, if it was a snow spell, the air could release its magic.

Georgia held her breath as the piece of orb twirled in the sky like a dandelion. It bobbed up and down, wandering aimlessly in the air. Dane must've gotten impatient, for he zapped it with a line of magic.

The orb exploded into a shower of fireworks that sprayed the ground.

Georgia smirked. "Good going."

Dane shrugged. "I was only trying to get it to do something."

"Well, you trying to get it to do something caused it to explode."

"How was I supposed to know?"

"This could be a dangerous spell. We can't act irresponsibly toward it."

He nodded bashfully. "Right. Sorry. I'll try again." This time Dane let the spell bob and waver for a full minute before he turned to Georgia. "I think it's safe to say that this isn't an atmospheric spell."

"I think you're right." She tapped her chin in thought. "Okay, so that didn't work. What's next?"

"We work it into the ground."

That's how it went with attempting to decipher unknown spells. Use the world around you to hone down on unknown magical properties and then continue to narrow how you work a spell until it finally gave up its secrets.

Dane broke off another sliver of orb and let it fall to the earth. It sat still for a moment, like a drop of water, but then ever so slowly, it sank into the ground as if the earth was drinking it up.

Georgia held her breath, waiting for whatever would happen next. Finally, after several long seconds, the dried-up husk that was left of last year's crop slowly turned from brown to yellow.

"I think we've got something," Dane whispered.

Magic pushed out of the ground like a vine. Sparkles and fireflies of power wrapped around brown blades of grass and coaxed them up like beanstalks. The magic seemed to pull and tug, wanting them to grow. Ever so slowly the vegetation followed suit. It was timid, uncoiling at a snail's pace. But as the power wound round the stem, the yellow grass became a vibrant green. Leaves unfurled from the stalk as it stretched toward the sky. Power shimmered, cocooning around it protectively as it grew. It elongated until finally the stalk fully formed into a rope of corn, replete with tassels on top.

Georgia exhaled a breath. "Would you look at that?"

Dane nodded. "Not what I expected."

She frowned. "What did you expect?"

"I don't know." He scratched his head. "Something, but not that."

Georgia inspected the vegetable. She ran her fingers down the stalk. "It's not a mirage. It's real." She snapped off a leaf. "See?"

He took the leaf she handed him. "Yeah, I see that."

He had sounded disappointed, so Georgia said, "What is it? What's wrong?"

"I don't know. Doesn't it seem a little…strange to you?"

"Does what seem strange?"

He pointed to the corn. "That. This. Doesn't it seem strange that the spell brings vegetation back to life?"

"No. I mean, I don't know. Does it seem that way to you?"

Dane shifted his weight from side to side. "Yeah, it does. If I had an arcane spell that according to Donalbain was sought after, I'd want it to do more than simply grow a corn stalk."

"I'm sure it does do more than that," she said. "But we're just out here in the middle of a cornfield testing it. If you took it somewhere else, you might get different results."

"You're only saying that to make me feel better."

She nodded. "I am. That's true."

Georgia expected him to laugh, but Dane didn't. Instead he stared at the corn. "This is one thing that the spell does, but it isn't the only thing."

"It made vegetation grow."

He shook his head. "No, you're not seeing it correctly."

She bristled. "I resent that."

His tone became apologetic. "What I mean is, yes, it did make it grow, but how did it do it?"

That's when Georgia realized what Dane was suggesting. "It brought the vegetation back to life."

"Bingo!" He snapped his fingers. "It took what was dried-up and dead and gave it life. That's what it did. It didn't sprout a new seed. At least not that I saw. Instead it rejuvenated it. In fact, the spell reconstructed and replenished it."

He was right. That was exactly what had happened. "But you're concerned."

"Of course I am. I have a hard time believing that Gator wants to end world hunger."

"But that's what this spell could do."

"But that's not what he wants it for," Dane told her. "It doesn't fit with the narrative that we know about him."

Georgia scoffed. "Okay, what *do* we know about this criminal that we actually know nothing about?"

"Well, we know he hired Donalbain to find the spell, but even Donalbain doesn't know what it does. If this orb"—he lifted the mason jar—"was simply going to replenish wheat fields, Donalbain would've known that. Gator would've told him. Why wouldn't he have? There would have been no reason not to. But Gator didn't tell Donalbain anything. And here we are in a cornfield using the spell and finding out that it grows vegetation. But I don't think that's all." Dane flashed their light around the field. "You hear all those crickets?"

"How can I not? They're loud."

"Let's catch some."

"What? Do they bite?"

He rolled his eyes. "They don't bite. Come on. Help me grab a couple."

How had this night gone from growing corn to suddenly searching for fishing bait? Georgia grumbled but did her best to help Dane catch a couple of crickets.

The crickets, on the other hand, had not received the memo that they were to be caught. They remained elusive, jumping out of reach at almost every turn.

Finally Dane was so frustrated that he chanted a capture spell. Within seconds, half a dozen crickets filled his hand.

"I should have done that in the first place," he grumbled.

"What? You didn't like the workout that you were getting?" Georgia teased.

He glared at her. "Very funny. Okay. Now here goes."

"What are you going—"

But before she could get the question out, Dane squished the crickets between both hands. Georgia recoiled. "Ew. Why'd you do that?"

"Just a hunch," he said, dropping the carcasses on the ground.

"Those poor little crickets," she mused. "They had no idea just being around you would be deadly."

From his squatted position on the ground, Dane looked up at her. "If I'm right, they won't be dead long."

He took what remained of the first orb and dropped it on the cricket's lifeless bodies. The magic sat atop the corpses for a few seconds before sliding like raindrops into them and disappearing.

For several moments nothing happened. Georgia was about to theorize that her husband had gone certifiably nuts, but just as she was about to say something, one of the bodies twitched.

"That's right," Dane whispered.

The cricket shuddered and shook. Its leg had fallen off when Dane crushed it, and it lay a couple of inches from the body. Ever so slowly the leg was pulled by an invisible force to the insect's abdomen and sutured back into place with the help of a tendril of magic.

The other crickets lurched and quaked as if they were receiving electrical impulses. Their bodies quivered as they slowly came back to life.

Georgia sucked air. What in the world? Watching corn grow was one thing. Seeing insects be healed and given breath again was quite another.

After a full minute the crickets stopped shuddering. They stood motionless for a moment, but when Dane reached to grab them, they jumped off, disappearing into the barren cornfield.

Georgia's jaw dropped. "What just happened?"

Of course she knew what had just happened, but she wanted to hear Dane's take on it. He cleared his throat and stared into the night.

"We just witnessed the orb bringing crickets back to life."

"And what does this mean? I mean, really?" Georgia asked.

Darkness filled Dane's eyes. He stared into the distance for a long moment before replying, "I'm afraid that if the orb can do that to crickets, it can do that to things that are much, much bigger."

"Like?" she asked even though she knew the answer.

"Like humans." His gaze locked on hers. "That the orb has the capability of bringing humans back from the dead."

CHAPTER 16

They were silent on the way home, both of them digesting the weight of what they'd observed. Because it was the best way she knew to work out problems, Georgia talked to calm the heaviness of their discovery.

"Just because you brought crickets back to life doesn't mean it can do the same to humans."

Dane gave her a hard look. "Yes, it does. I know that you don't want to think that the spell is that powerful. But we're talking about arcane knowledge. The possibility of what it's capable of is great. It can bring back the dead. Gator could raise an army and have them do whatever he wants."

"So how do we move forward?" she asked. "Do we run to the council and tell them?"

Dane was quiet. "I don't know. I need to think about it. Yes, the council needs to know what's going on. That's true. But if this sort of information got out, there are a lot of bad guys who would go to great lengths to have this power. We've got to be careful."

Georgia agreed. They needed to keep this information to themselves as long as they could.

Dane squeezed her hand. "We'll figure it out. For now, let's lock it up and get some rest. Okay?"

"Okay."

They pulled into the garage and found Rose slumbering on the couch. She startled when Georgia woke her. "Want Dane to drive you home?"

Rose shook her head. "No, dear. I'll be fine. Everything go okay?"

Georgia nodded. "It did. Thank you for watching Judy. I hope she wasn't any trouble."

"Not at all." Rose got up and shouldered her handbag. "She's a treat to watch. I'd be happy to come again anytime."

"Thank you."

"You're very welcome." She shuffled to the door. "I'll see you first thing in the morning."

"Okay. You sure that you're all right to drive?"

Rose batted her away with a hand. "I'm fine. I'm not so old that I can't see at night. Tally-ho!"

Georgia waved and shut the door. She checked on Judy while Dane put the spell back in the basement. Their daughter slept soundly. Georgia readied for bed, changed her clothes and washed her face and brushed her teeth. By the time she was slipping under the covers, Dane entered the room.

"Everything secure?" she asked.

He nodded. "It's all locked up. We can discuss with Brad and Rose what to do tomorrow. But for now, let's sleep on it, see if any of the answers will come to us in our slumbers."

"I know one answer—keep the spell away from Garryn."

Dane scowled. "He's not a bad guy."

She shrugged. "So you say."

"At some point you have to listen to me on this."

"Not sure that I do."

"I'm pretty sure that you do. We are married, and if we want to have a wonderful happily married life, we need to listen to each other."

Georgia splayed a hand over her chest. "I do listen to you. I listen to you a lot. It's just that on this subject I am going to agree to disagree."

He shook his head. "Just don't let your warped personal opinions about Garryn get in the way of our mission."

"You mean the mission to find out that he's the Gator?"

Dane pressed his fingers to his closed eyes in frustration. "Yes, that mission. Georgia, I know that you don't trust him. But right now we have to. We don't have any other choice. He's our leader in this. He's only helped us. It was his office who gave us the intelligence to find Donalbain."

She quirked a brow. "See? Suspicious right there. You're only digging a hole. You realize that, don't you? The more you keep saying that Garryn has nothing to do with this, the more guilty you actually make him look."

Dane shook his head and sat on the bed. The mattress sank deep under his weight. Her husband wore nothing but low-slung pajama pants. He ran a hand down his bicep. Georgia couldn't help but admire his well-defined chest. Dane was all cut muscle—hard, solid and strong.

Whereas she was soft and round in places that she didn't like to think about. Her butt wasn't nearly as high as it used to be, and neither were her boobs for that matter. The last time she'd looked in the mirror, she seriously considered getting a boob job. Every time she saw them, she thought about the song, "Do Your Ears Hang Low." Only instead of ears, she replaced it with boobs. Because yes, hers did hang low and they certainly wallowed to and fro and she figured that if they kept sagging, she would most definitely be able to tie them in a knot and a bow.

What a depressing thought.

But Dane, he was like most men in that age became him. His forties looked good on him. But for Georgia she felt like her thirties had looked great on her and her forties were a mess. It was all downhill from there, she figured.

Dane said something, but she was so in her own head that she didn't hear him. "What was that?"

He sighed. "Do you think that you can put your mistrust of Garryn aside? We have no proof that he's untrustworthy. And we need him as an ally."

She shrugged. "Okay. We need him as an ally."

He tipped his chin down at her. "What's going on with you? Why are you so convinced that he's our Gator?"

Georgia didn't have an answer.

Dane ran a finger down her arm. "Is this about Claudia? I know you're worried about her. So am I."

Georgia didn't know what she would do without her sister—if anything happened to her. She had forced herself not to think about it too much. It was way too painful. But the truth was, her sister could very well be sick. Claudia could have cancer. Georgia would have to be strong for Claudia, show a solid front. But in reality she didn't know how easy it would be for her to act like everything was okay.

Claudia was who she shared all her worries with. If something bothered Georgia, she turned to her sister for guidance. But this time Claudia needed Georgia to be strong. It was time for her to have to lean on Georgia. That was for sure. Georgia was up for the task, but it still didn't make it any easier to deal with.

"I...I don't know what I'd do if something happened to her," Georgia admitted.

"Come here." Dane opened his arms, and Georgia scooted into them, resting her head on his strong shoulder. "I know that you're scared right now. I'm sure Claudia is, too. But you can't let that fear turn other things sour. You're looking for things to distract you. And you've found one of them in this whole Garryn thing. You want reasons to suspect him. But Georgia, that's not helping either of us. We have found a very serious spell, one that has grave potential to be a real threat in this life. At some point the council will have to know about that. We need their help tracking down Gator."

She pulled back and glanced up at him. "I know, it's just...I don't know. I feel like everything is upside down and I don't know which way is up. I feel like we're supposed to trust the wizard council, but I'm having a hard time with that. I'm also having a hard time with Claudia."

"Why don't you take a break?"

She stared at him. "What'ch you talking about, Dane?"

He shrugged. "Just that. Taking a break. Give yourself a little bit of downtime. I can do some of this without you, you know. You don't have to be super involved."

She bristled. "This is our company."

"Yes," he said soothingly. "It is. It's the two of us. But you're worried about your sister, and rightly so. Maybe you just need time off. I'm not saying take a whole month. All I'm suggesting is giving yourself some breathing room. Take tomorrow. Go spend it with Claudia. Eat ice cream and shop. There's nothing here that can't last until you get back."

She thought about that. Maybe she was getting too deep into things. After all, she was digging up dirt on a council leader and was convincing herself that he was the Gator. Georgia must've lost her mind. Of course Garryn wasn't a bad guy. He couldn't be. Down in her subconscious, she knew that. But the discomforting facts kept pushing up into her conscious mind, making her rethink what she knew.

Perhaps Dane was right. She needed a break. She needed to take a day away from work and relax. After all, she was dealing with some heavy stuff—her sister's health, a spell that could potentially raise the dead. That was a lot for one person to swallow. Not only that, but there were her duties with the PTO. The book fair was coming up soon, and she'd have to dress up like Candy the Cat for it.

There was a lot going on, that much was the truth. It wouldn't kill her to simply take a day for herself. Besides, it would be good to spend some time with Claudia. Claudia would probably welcome the idea.

"Let me see if my sister's free tomorrow," she said.

"That's the spirit," Dane replied. "Go and do fun stuff with her."

She grabbed her phone from the nightstand and texted Claudia. *Hey girl, are you free tomorrow? Want to spend the day shopping?*

Claudia replied within seconds. *Sounds like a plan. You buying me a new outfit? I could really use one.*

Georgia chuckled. *Sure thing. Whatever you want. I hear rainbow sequins are in this season.*

Claudia sent back an emoji face with its tongue sticking out.

"Okay," she told Dane, who had sunk under the covers. "We're on for tomorrow."

"Good. See? You'll be feeling better in no time."

"I hope so."

"I know you will." He turned toward her and smiled. "You need to get your mind off all this, at least for a little while. It's not good for you to be creating fantasies."

She scoffed. "I'll have you know that I'm most certainly not creating any fantasies. Everything I think is based on fact."

"Strange facts," he joked.

She poked him in the ribs. "I don't appreciate that."

He rested his hand on her belly and started making slow circles. "I love that you get worked up about strange facts. It's one of the reasons I married you."

She shook her head in annoyance. "Sure it is."

"It is." Dane leaned over and kissed her. "Now. Would you like to get some rest? We both have a full day ahead of us."

She nodded. "Yeah. Let's get some sleep."

Georgia sank down beside Dane. He snapped off the light and hugged her. "I love you."

"I love you," she murmured.

They kissed and she rolled to her side because she needed her personal space, and he liked his as well. Georgia had just closed her eyes when she heard a branch snap.

Dane bolted up.

"What is it?" she asked, her heart suddenly beating like mad.

He whipped off the covers. "It's the booby trap outside. It's gone off. Someone's here."

CHAPTER 17

Georgia jumped out of bed.

"What are you doing?" Dane asked.

A sliver of moonlight sliced through the blinds into the room, casting just enough light that she could make out Dane's worried expression.

She looked around as if he'd asked her a trick question. "What do you mean, what am I doing? I'm going out to help you capture whoever's out there."

"No, you're not," he said emphatically.

She pulled on pants. "Yes, I am."

"Darn it, Georgia. Can you for once listen to what it is I want you to do?"

"I'll have you know that I have listened to you. I'm taking off tomorrow. But this isn't tomorrow. This is today and as far as I'm concerned, I'm on the clock."

He slipped into a pair of sneakers. "You're not going outside. Judy's upstairs. Someone needs to protect her."

"Someone also needs to protect you. I can be back in Judy's room with the casting of one spell if I need to. I'll make sure of it. But I'm not letting you go out there by yourself. Not after what happened before."

Worry flashed across his face. He knew she was right. Also, Georgia would sooner die than let anything happen to Judy. Dane knew that, too.

He gave a nod. "Come on. Let's hurry."

They raced to the back door, and Dane slowly opened it. "Stay close."

"What if they're headed to the front door?"

He scowled. "We need to sneak up on them."

"What if they break the front door down?"

His words came out bright and angry. "Do you want to stay inside or come with me?"

"I'm coming with you," she relented.

The night was still when they stepped into it. Not even the sound of crickets filled the air. It was as if nature knew that it needed to be quiet, and so it was being perfectly still.

It was late and most of the lights were off in the neighboring houses. Dane cut silently through the grass. Georgia stayed as close to him as she dared.

The lamps from the street cast strange shadows on the house. For the first time Georgia noticed that wow, they sure did have some very large hedge bushes lining their home. It would be super easy for anyone to simply hide behind them and then jump out when a person was least suspecting it.

Dane pointed to the ground. There sat a couple of cans and a string. She frowned. Was that the booby trap he had laid? She figured he would have used magic to put down a trap. But that looked like Dane had dusted off his Boy Scout trapping guide and looked for the silliest not-quite-a-snare imaginable.

She wrinkled her brow at him as if to say, *Did you really make that?*

He shrugged as if to reply, *It worked, didn't it?*

She followed him because she supposed that it had worked. But every time she stepped on the grass, it sounded loud as a gunshot to her. She just knew whoever was hiding was lying in wait for them.

Georgia nibbled her bottom lip and kept her hands clenched, ready to counterattack if need be.

Dane reached one corner of the house. He signaled for her to listen. She cocked an ear toward him, and that's when she heard what seemed like a scraping sound.

Her eyes widened. There *was* someone there. They were just around the corner, up a little ways. Her heart hammered, and sweat poured from her palms. She wiped the slick off them, onto her clothes. But as soon as she dried her hands, they simply started pouring again.

Deciding that she'd just have to deal with it, Georgia closed the distance to Dane and crept behind him as he rounded the house and headed toward the sound.

She held her breath as they closed in. A scraping noise came from behind one of the gigantic hedges. Why did they have such large hedges? Wasn't that like an insurance liability? Why hadn't Dane ever trimmed them? Why had Georgia only just noticed how absolutely terrifying they were? Why had she only just been made aware of that now, when she was outside looking for a creeper who was trying to break into her house?

Dane stopped a few feet away from the hedge. Still it continued. *Scrape, scrape, scrape.*

It sounded like someone was taking a paint peeler to the window frame, trying to jimmy it up. Fear bolted down her body, pulsing all the way to her toes. They needed to stop whoever it was before they broke into the house.

Dane quick glanced around and saw a stick lying on the grass. He plucked it up and held it like a baseball bat.

The stick looked like dead wood to her. It would probably break when it made contact with the intruder's back. But Georgia was ready with her magic.

She curled her hands to fists and waited. Dane gave her a nod, and then he charged into the hedge.

"Get out of here," he yelled.

But no person yelled back. Instead, something growled. Growled? What the heck was in there? The hedge swayed and then something hissed.

Dane jumped away, and scurrying behind him came a raccoon. The creature vaulted onto the grass and lifted its arms like it was about to do some sort of karate move, then it bared its teeth, hissed and ran off into the night.

Georgia's mouth dropped. Dane pulled leaves from his hair. "Are you okay?" she asked.

He exhaled a deep breath and inspected his arms and shoulders. "I don't think I was bitten. Was I?"

She ran her fingers over his skin. "No. You're just scraped a little. It looks like from the hedge. I don't see any teeth marks. What happened?"

Dane raked his fingers through his hair. "I think I interrupted the raccoon while it was eating. It must've gotten in the trash and then came over here to enjoy its meal."

She exhaled a sigh of relief. "I'm just glad that you're okay."

He smiled weakly. "Me too." Dane wrapped an arm around her shoulders. "Come on. Let's go inside and make sure I don't have to get a rabies shot."

"Okay."

They'd turned to go back to the house when a crash came, sounding like a tree had fallen into a pit of empty tin cans. Georgia jumped up, and Dane pushed her behind him.

"It's another trap."

"Did the raccoon sneak back?"

He shook his head. "No. That sounded too big. Come on."

They rushed to the other side of the house with Dane keeping Georgia behind him. When they reached one of the hedges, the tree was waving as if someone was stuck in it.

"Don't try to struggle," Dane commanded. "It'll only make the trap worse. Sit still and I'll have you out in a minute."

Wow. He was a lot nicer than Georgia would've been. "Do you have a light?" he asked her.

Georgia pulled her phone from her pocket and thumbed on the flashlight. The hedge was tangled up in a mess of string. It looked like someone had been trying to decorate for Christmas but had wound up decorating for Halloween instead.

Lashed to the string was a body. She made out feet and legs, and even the person's booty. They were bent over, facedown, tied to the tree. If Georgia's heart hadn't been hammering so badly, she was pretty sure that tears of laughter would've been leaking from her eyes.

The person struggled. "Please don't hurt me."

"I won't if you don't do anything stupid," Dane said. "Just hold still and I'll have you out."

The intruder remained motionless while Dane used magic to snip the string from the body. By the time he was done, there was a pile of white tendrils on the ground that looked more like worms that thread, Georgia decided.

"Are there any more of you?" she asked.

"No," the man replied. "Listen, I can explain."

"I think you'd better. Georgia, have the light ready," Dane commanded.

Georgia lifted the light and shone it where the man's face would be. Except she was still looking at his backside—the hair on his head, to be precise.

Dane slowly hoisted the man around, and when his face came into view, Georgia gasped.

She could not believe her eyes. Surely she was mistaken. Georgia blinked several times, hoping it would help. But no. The man's appearance did not change.

Finally she whispered, "Principal Brock? What are you doing here?"

He adjusted his glasses. "I *can* explain. I wasn't lying when I said that. Please. Don't call the police. Give me a chance to tell you everything. I promise that you'll understand once you've heard my story."

Georgia's gaze flickered to Dane, whose jaw twitched. "All right. We'll listen. But this better be good. Otherwise I'll be calling the wizard council about this, and someone will haul you off to jail tonight."

CHAPTER 18

"Tell us everything," Dane growled when they were inside.

Georgia didn't blame him for his anger. Thanks to Stan Brock sneaking around outside of their home, Georgia and Dane had been worried, scared. Not only that, but they had been fearful something could have happened to Judy.

His actions had put them on alert. Georgia's nerve endings were an absolute mess. She was a coiled bundle, ready to strike.

Stan took a seat in their kitchen. He pushed his glasses up his nose nervously. Leaves stuck out of his hair, and dirt smudged his shirt. Whatever his excuse was, it better be good, Georgia thought. There was no reason for him to have done what he had.

"Talk," Dane commanded.

Stan cleared his throat. "Your wife knows that I have a book on arcane spells."

Dane's brows shot up at that. His gaze darted to Georgia. "She does, does she?"

Oh, that was right. Georgia had not actually told Dane about the book. Well, could he blame her? She'd been pretty darn busy this past day, what with helping him turn dead crickets into live ones. He could deal with it.

But as way of apology, she did shrug. "Sorry. I was going to mention it."

He said nothing, just turned his attention back to Stan. That made her bristle a bit, but Georgia bit her frustration back down. "What about the book?" her husband asked Stan.

"I had a bad relative, one who spliced spells to himself. He was able to harness a lot of power, and the power got passed down the line."

Dane crossed his arms and sat in a chair. "It became part of your genetic makeup?"

Stan nodded. "Exactly."

"How?"

He shook his head. "The magic fused to his DNA." The principal looked at Georgia. "Your wife really didn't tell you any of this?"

"I've been busy," Georgia fumed. "Listen, I should have. I was going to, but I just got really, really busy. Okay. Let's hash it out, then. Dane, Principal Brock has magic because his grandfather liked to play with spells. He played with them so much that they fused to him. He became a super sort of wizard. But what no one realized was that the talent would be passed from generation to generation. Hence, Principal Brock is a grim reaper. But as much as that explains the fact of your current existence, it doesn't explain exactly what you were doing snooping around our yard in the middle of the night." Both Dane and the principal stared at her, mouths open. Georgia shook her head in annoyance. "What? You were both acting like I should have said something, so I did. I said a lot. Now. Please continue."

Stan wrung his hands. "Well, um, you found my book of arcane spells and returned it to me. From the way you talked, I had a feeling that y'all two may or may not have an arcane—or as I like to refer to them, *dangerous*—spell here somewhere. Look, you have to understand that my grandfather tampering with restricted magic changed all of us. Because of his actions, my family will never be the same again. So of course I was worried that you might have something here that's deadly, or at least can wreak havoc, the sort that you don't want in your lives."

Dane studied him. "So what were you going to do?"

Stan's gaze cut to the floor. "Well, I was going to see if I could find it and rescue it from you."

"You were going to steal it."

"I was doing it for your own good. I don't want anyone to get hurt."

"*You* could have gotten hurt," Dane snapped. "Sneaking around in our yard could have gotten you very hurt."

Stan shielded his eyes for a moment. "My grandfather accidentally used his grim reaper's powers on my grandmother."

Georgia's heart hurt for him. She sat down beside Stan and covered his hand with hers. "I'm so sorry."

He nodded. "She didn't go quickly. She went slowly. It took days for her to fully transition to the other side. When she finally did slip out of this world, she looked like a ghost, just a thin apparition that finally dissolved into nothing."

"Oh no," she said, her heart breaking. "I can understand why you came here."

Stan looked up at her with hope in his eyes. "You can?"

"Sure. You're worried that we would do something irresponsible with the spell. Well, that's not our intention. We now know what it does. What it is."

Hope flared in his eyes. "You do?"

Dane shot Georgia a warning look. He wasn't sure how much to tell Stan. It was obvious. The spell was strong. If it was capable of doing what they thought, anyway. The repercussions of it could be felt around the entire world if the orb got into the wrong hands.

"What does it do?" the principal asked. He glanced at Dane, who scowled, and he quickly added, "If you want to tell me, that is. Let me assure you, I don't want the orb. I only want to keep people safe. After what happened to my family, you can understand that."

Georgia could understand that. She could understand very well indeed. But could Dane?

She met his gaze, and Dane rubbed a thumb across his jawline in thought. He sighed. "The spell is powerful. We think it may have healing properties."

Stan took in what Dane said, drumming his fingers on the table. "Those old arcane spells could really heal. That's good. Very helpful sort of orb." He smiled. His gaze washed from Georgia, who was smirking, and Dane, who was avoiding looking at his wife. Stan continued. "But that's not all it does, is it?"

Georgia spoke. "Let's just say it has *very strong* healing potential. My husband is being conservative in his estimation."

Stan paused and then said, "You need to get rid of it."

Dane's gaze flashed to him. "What? Why?"

"Because wherever these spells tend to turn up, bad things happen. If the wrong person finds out what you have, they will stop at nothing to get it. If my grandfather was still alive, he would have torn this house apart to find what you're hiding. The spells are not to be trifled with. Trust me. What I'm saying, I'm doing so for your own good. I'm trying to help you."

"I appreciate it," Dane said, sighing and rising from the chair. "You've been a big help in telling us what to expect."

Georgia stared at Dane. He was just going to dismiss Principal Brock as if what he had to say didn't matter, as if he didn't have anything important to tell them. He had told them critical details. Granted, they pretty much already knew that someone wanted this spell, namely Gator. So in that there wasn't anything new.

But clearly Stan wanted to help them, and it would be silly for them to refuse that. They still didn't know who Gator was, and that put them at a great disadvantage.

Dane gestured to Stan that it was time for him to leave. The principal rose but stopped. "What I've found out in my life is that there are plenty of people who will pretend to be on your side. A lot of folks. My intelligence sources are hinting that someone who is supposed to be helping you is actually doing the opposite."

Dane smirked. "Your intelligence sources?"

Stan nodded. "That's right. You can't be a grim reaper and not have connections."

The look in Dane's eyes suggested that he didn't believe the principal. "Well, thank you for helping us. I appreciate it. Now. My wife and I are very tired. We'd like to get some rest."

Stan walked to the door and stopped. "If you don't hear anything else I say, listen to this—I have it on good authority that someone on the council is working against us. They're not on the side of good. Be careful who you trust. Because if you put your faith in the wrong person, you could wind up dead."

With that, Stan pushed up his glasses and opened the door. "Good night. Stay alert out there."

After he disappeared into the darkness, Georgia turned to Dane. "Well, I wonder if his sources are suggesting that Garryn is the bad guy?"

He rolled his eyes. "Not now, Georgia. We don't even know if we can trust the principal. He might not even be a grim reaper."

As they headed off to bed, Georgia had a feeling that Stan was in fact a grim reaper and that everything he had told them was true.

Which meant that she and Dane needed to stay alert and watch their backs.

CHAPTER 19

The next day Georgia showed up to Claudia's house bright and early with coffee.

Claudia answered on the first ring, and Georgia held up a paper cup. "Fuel for the road?"

"You know it," Claudia said, took the cup and had a large sip. "Caramel macchiato, my favorite. Hmmm. This is heaven. Thank you."

"You're very welcome. I thought you could use some jet fuel since we've got a little ways to drive."

Claudia arched a perfectly penciled brown brow. "Oh? Where *are* we going?"

"The unclaimed baggage place."

Claudia squealed. "Oh my gosh. I haven't been there in ages. Oh, what a treat. I've been needing a new wedding dress."

Georgia snorted. "Okay. Well. I hope that's a joke."

"It is." Claudia shut her door and locked it. "I'm never getting married again unless he's rich with a heart condition."

Georgia laughed. "I'm sure we could find that man for you, and the best part is that we wouldn't even have to look too far."

It was Claudia's turn to chuckle. She snaked her arm through Georgia's. "Okay. Let's go."

It took a couple of hours to reach the store. The entire drive over, both women managed to not talk about the biopsy results that they were still waiting on. Claudia seemed in good spirits, pointing out the scenery and making jokes. But Georgia wondered if that was just for show and if Claudia was really hurting on the inside.

It would be like Claudia to do that. She was a fierce protector of Georgia, the sort that punched kids on the playground who messed with her when they were kids. She projected an image of strength, and even now, when Georgia knew that Claudia was worried, she was still cracking jokes and trying to have a good time.

They arrived a few minutes after the store opened. Claudia grabbed Georgia's arm. "Wow. I've forgotten how awesome this place is."

It was awesome. The store acquired its merchandise by buying up unclaimed baggage from airlines. Then they sorted through the bags, which held all sorts of things—electronics, clothes, toys and more—and they resold them to the public. Diving into the store was like hunting in the best bargain shops. You never knew what sort of treasures you would find.

"I could use a new dress," Georgia said.

"Me too. Something that makes me feel beautiful. Come on. Let's shop."

They spent the next hour sorting through clothes and electronics. Georgia found a peach-colored dress that would be perfect for church, and Claudia found dresses that would be suitable for a beach vacation—airy and in bright, cheerful colors.

"Your wardrobe picks are so much brighter than mine," Georgia moped.

Claudia laughed. "Come on. Let's find you something fun."

With Claudia taking charge, they scanned the racks. "How about this?" she asked, holding up a red dress with a large keyhole cut out in the back.

"That's pretty," Georgia said, unsure about it. Where would she wear it? She and Dane didn't have time for dates.

Claudia threw it into her arms. "Try it on. And how about this?" She hoisted a slinky black dress onto her elbow. "Try this one, too. And this one."

By the time they were heading into the changing rooms, Georgia had an armful of clothes. Though the red dress didn't work out, the peach church dress and a blue sundress did.

"Let's see," Claudia said.

Georgia stepped out of the room wearing the blue sundress. Claudia wore a green over-the-shoulder dress. She whistled. "You look great in that, Mama."

Georgia laughed. "You think so?"

"I know so. You'd better get it. It's a steal."

"I don't know," she wavered.

Claudia wagged a finger at her. "If you don't, I'm buying a wedding dress. I swear it."

"Okay," she said through chuckles. "I'll buy it. Just so you don't purchase a wedding gown. I know what'll happen then."

"What's that?"

"You'll end up searching for the millionaire with the heart condition."

Claudia smiled. "You got that right. I'm hungry. How long have we been here?"

Georgia glanced at her watch. "About two hours."

"Already?"

"Yep."

"Well, I'm starved. Let's grab some lunch."

They found a cute little sandwich shop a few miles away and ordered light feminine finger sandwiches and drank glasses of tea.

Claudia stared at her glass while they waited for the food. "Thanks for taking me out today. I needed it."

Georgia contemplated her sister. "I wish there was more that I could do."

Claudia took Georgia's hand. "You've already done so much. You have no idea. Just bringing me out here has lifted my spirits. The waiting…"

Her eyes brimmed with tears, and Georgia squeezed her hand. "I'm so sorry. The waiting is the worst, I'm sure."

Claudia pulled a tissue from her purse and dabbed her eyes. "It's a killer. I thought for sure that I'd have an answer by now. Whether it's good or bad, I don't care. I just want to know what it is." A tear streaked down her cheek before she had a chance to dry it with her tissue. "I can handle knowing whatever the outcome is, it's just I thought that I'd be better at waiting. But I just haven't been. I even called one of my exes."

Georgia's jaw dropped. "You did what?"

Claudia showed her sister her palm. "Don't get excited. I only called an old boyfriend—Clay."

"Clay? Didn't you find out that he was dealing drugs?"

"Yeah. He's turned his life around since then."

"Since his drug-dealing days?"

Claudia dismissed her with a wave. "That was ten years ago. He was only dealing to save up some money. He did that and started a business."

"Let me guess—another drug-dealing business?"

Claudia scoffed. "No. Well, actually I don't know. He didn't say."

"Don't you think that should be a red flag?"

"Not really."

And as awesome as Claudia was, there was also this side to her—the side that freaked out and then made very rash decisions. Clay had indeed been a drug dealer. He's almost gotten Claudia severely injured.

"Don't you remember when those guys with guns came to his door that one night when you were there?" Georgia reminded her. "You were scared to death."

"They had the wrong house," Claudia said. "It was an honest mistake."

Georgia shot her a dark look. "Oh, the wrong house? How many drug dealers lived in his neighborhood?"

She shrugged. "I really don't know. But once they saw Clay through the window, they realized that they had the wrong man and left."

"I just don't think it's a good idea to be talking to him right now. Not while you're…"

"Compromised?" Claudia said, annoyed. "You might be my little sister, but you don't have to protect me."

"I'm not trying to protect you." She paused. "Okay, maybe I am. But I'm protecting you from dating some guy who you broke up with for good reasons. He might have changed, maybe. But Clay could also be lying. Once a drug dealer, always a drug dealer."

"It was just pot, Georgia. It's not like he was out there peddling Fentanyl."

"Thank goodness for that small mercy." She stared at her sister's face all bunched up in frustration. "Look, I know you're scared. I am, too. But I don't think that jumping back into a relationship with a guy who caused you a lot of grief is a way to deal with what's going on now."

"It's just…" Tears streamed down her cheeks. "It's just that I feel very mortal right now, Georgia. I feel raw, like I'm not in control of anything. I wish that I was like you, had your gifts. That power, that gift that you have, it is a blessing. It makes you feel like you can do anything. At least, it makes me see you that way. But here I am, a victim to my own body. I'm at the mercy of waiting to hear the news—whether it be good or bad—and until then I can't help it if I'm thinking of men that I used to have a relationship with. I'm doing whatever I can to distract myself because I'm going crazy just thinking about it. If I have cancer and have to go through chemo, how is that going to be?"

"I'll be with you," Georgia told her. "You won't go through this alone. You know that."

"I know." Her gaze dropped to the table. "It's just sometimes I wish that there was more that I had. That I wasn't a burden on you."

"You're not a burden," Georgia said. "I don't want you to think that. Do I make you feel that way?"

"No, you don't. *Not at all.* I guess it's just my own guilt. You have a family and other responsibilities. I feel bad taking you away from those things."

"You're not taking me away from them," Georgia insisted. "You are my family, and family is the most important thing that we have. If you don't have family, what have you got? Nothing. I want to be here for you. You are not a burden. Not in the least. I'm thankful that I could take you to the hospital. That makes me feel grateful." She sighed, rubbed her forehead. "Look, I'm not going to say that I know what you're going through. All I'm saying is that drudging up old boyfriends from the past—ones who almost got you shot and killed because of their chosen profession, if you can call it that—is not a great idea."

"Even if he's hot?" Claudia joked.

It took everything she had for Georgia not to crack a smile. "Even if he is hot. Boyfriends that put my sister in bodily danger are big no-no's. I don't care how rich they are, how perfect their bodies are, or even how much hair they've got."

"Clay does have a lot of hair." Georgia shot her a venomous look. Claudia lifted her hands in surrender. "Okay. Okay. I won't talk to him anymore."

"Do you promise?" Claudia pretended to consider it. Georgia growled, "Claudia?"

"Yes, I promise," she teased. "I just like to worry you a little, that's all. It's entertaining and I need something to make me laugh."

"How about you find it in someone else. I really don't need to have a heart attack when I'm trying to simply get through the next few days."

"Okay," Claudia said glumly.

"Speaking of next few days, when will they have the results of your biopsy?"

"Any day now," she said. "I should be getting a call any minute."

The waitress appeared with their plates and set them down. "Wow, this looks great," Georgia said.

Claudia spied the tomatoes peeking out from under a slice of bread. "Can I have your tomato?"

"I wanted to eat them both," Georgia said.

"Come on. I might be dying," she joked.

Georgia threw her napkin at her sister and then peeled back the bread so that Claudia could fish a tomato from one half of her sandwich. She tossed it in her mouth and moaned with pleasure. "Oh, that is good. Thank you."

Georgia lifted her sandwich to her mouth. "For that, you owe me."

Claudia laughed. "You can have anything of mine that you want."

Georgia didn't say it, but she thought that the only thing she wanted was for Claudia to be healthy. She said a silent prayer before eating, asking for just that.

CHAPTER 20

When she got back to the house, Georgia was fifty dollars lighter but an armload of clothes heavier. She dropped her bag on the kitchen table. "I'm home!"

Rose shuffled into the room. "Oh, you're back. How was your morning with your sister? Did the two of you have a grand time shopping until dropping?"

"We did, thank you." Georgia noticed how quiet the house was. "Where are Dane and Brad?"

"Oh, they went to get some lunch."

"They didn't take you?"

"Nah. I told them to bring me something back. I didn't want to be in a restaurant between them. Too much testosterone for me, I think. They would probably want to go to one of those Hooters places. That's not the type of establishment that I like to patron."

Georgia bit back a laugh. "There isn't a Hooters around here."

Rose shrugged. "Doesn't mean it'll stop them."

"No, I suppose not." Georgia laid her purse atop the counter. "So how did things go today?"

Rose crossed over and pulled out a chair. "I suppose it went just fine. Dane said there had been a breakthrough with the spell, but he was still researching it."

Ah, so he wanted to make sure that when he told Brad and Rose about it, that he was one hundred percent right. "Did he tell you about our late-night visitor?"

Rose's brows shot up. "No, he didn't. What happened?"

So Georgia told Rose all about Principal Brock and how he had set off one of the booby traps and told them that they mustn't work with arcane spells.

"But the strangest thing he said was that there's someone in the wizard council who's not on our side."

"Oh, dear," Rose said glumly. "That doesn't sound good at all. Did he tell you who?"

"No, but I worry about Garryn."

"Why's that?" Georgia then proceeded to explain about finding him in the basement. "Did he steal anything?"

"Um, no. Not that I'm aware of."

Rose shrugged. "Could just be a misunderstanding."

"But that's not all. I found an article about him." She told Rose what she had learned when Garryn was the special prosecutor. "Don't you think that's suspicious?"

Rose rapped her fingers on the table. "Yes, I suppose it is. It does seem like Garryn might have some other interests going on."

"That's what I think, too."

"But if there's one thing that I've learned in my life, it's that it's best to trust someone until you have a reason not to trust them. And from what I've seen of Garryn, he's only been doing what he thinks is right to help you out."

"But don't you think it's a little strange that Stan Brock told us to watch out for one of the council members and here's Garryn acting all weird?"

"Not necessarily." Rose lifted from her chair and crossed to the fridge. "Would you like a glass of tea?"

"Sure. Thank you."

Rose poured two glasses and brought them back, setting one in front of Georgia. "Do you know how I got involved in all this wizard and witch drama?"

"No, I don't." Georgia sipped the tea. "Hmm. This is delicious. Just the right amount of sugar. Did you make it this morning?"

Rose plumped the base of her bun with her hand. "I most certainly did. A home should always have tea in it. In case visitors come over. You might not have cookies for them to snack on, but if you've got tea, you're doing pretty darn good."

Georgia couldn't help but laugh. "Wise words."

"I like to think so. But as I was saying, I was just a regular housewife, a regular woman my entire life. I never knew anything about your magical world until about ten years ago."

"You didn't?"

That surprised Georgia. Most people who were involved in magic and all things magical usually had grown up around it. It was rare that someone came into the world when they were older, and Rose *was old*. The fact that she had only discovered that magic existed on the planet was a shock.

"I did not know anything about the world until then, yes, and to be honest, I could have gone the rest of my life without knowing anything about it. But then my husband died."

Georgia reached for her hand and gloved it. "Oh no. I'm so sorry."

"He was the love of my life. We only had each other and loved each other ever since we had been teenagers. We weren't able to have children, even though we tried for years. It was the one thing that we weren't blessed with. Don't get me wrong," she quickly added, "I cherished every moment that I got to spend with my husband. I wouldn't take back any of it. He was the best thing that ever happened to me. For that, I'm grateful."

"So how did you find out about magic?"

Rose gave Georgia a little whimsical smile. "He left me a note. He'd written it before he passed with strict instructions not to open it until after he was gone. So I did, curious as to what he might have to tell me. I figured the message would be another love letter that I could add to my collection. But when I opened it, I was surprised to find that wasn't what it was at all."

"What was it?"

"It was a spell."

Georgia leaned forward, her interest piqued. "A spell? What sort?"

"It was a spell that when I read the enchantment, his face materialized. I tell you, the first time that happened, I nearly jumped out of my skin. I didn't know what to think. I was just a regular widow, minding my own business, reading this letter that my deceased husband had left me, and the next thing I knew, there he was, standing in my house!"

"That must've been quite a shock."

"You have no idea," Rose admitted. "I screamed when I saw him. I didn't know what to think. I may have fainted. I'm not sure. Wait. Now that I think about it, I did faint. I fell right on over out of my chair. I was lucky that I didn't wind up with a head injury."

Curious, Georgia asked, "What happened next?"

"Well, he started talking, and he explained that he had lived his entire life with magic. But because of the rules surrounding it, he hadn't been allowed to tell me, though he wished that he could have. He went on to say how much he loved me, but he felt guilty, terribly guilty for keeping such a secret from me for all those years. He said that if I wanted to learn more, there were people who would meet me."

Georgia watched as Rose stared off into the distance, her expression impossible to read. "That must've been quite a shock."

Rose nodded dumbly. "It was huge to think that my husband had kept that from me for so many years. Naturally I felt betrayed. There had been an entire part of his life that he'd kept from me. Why? Why had he done that? Oh, I understood the reason, but that didn't make it any easier to digest. I have realized that there are many things outside of our control. All I wanted was to have some of that control back. So after I got over the initial shock and confusion, I met with the people he suggested that I be introduced to." Her gaze met Georgia's. "They were old friends of my husband's and welcomed me with open arms. They told me what they could, and wished that they'd been able to talk with me sooner. They were happy just to say hello and have a supper with me, but they didn't understand that I wanted to know more."

Georgia quirked a brow. "More?"

"Yes. You have to realize that for forty years my husband had led a life that I knew nothing about. This was my chance to learn everything that I could. I wanted to understand not only why he'd kept that half of his life secret, but I wanted to understand the secrets in it."

"So what happened?" Georgia asked.

"They started to show me magic. They showed me some of his favorite spells and how to create a few. They showed me small things, a taste of power. But that wasn't enough for me. That's when I learned about spell hunters. They told me that there was an entire world of hidden spells, magical orbs that could do just about anything. You just had to know how to find them, of course. Not being magical myself, I had very little hope that I would indeed ever find any. But they put me in touch with covert companies that employed spell hunters. So I went back to work. In my seventies," she added with a laugh. "I walked into the workplace and started helping spell hunters. You see, it was the least that I could do to carry on my husband's name, to share a part of his life with him. He'd kept me from it when he was alive, but now that he was dead, I was learning everything about magic that I could.

"I became an advocate for magic. Once I saw what it could do, I realized that it can bring some wonder and hope to the world. Your sister, for instance, she may be sick. Magic could cure her."

Georgia nodded. "If she's sick, it could cure her, maybe. There are a lot of curing spells. It's an option."

Georgia had lucked out saving Dane. She didn't know if she could heal her sister.

"Do you see how you don't have to be afraid," Rose said. "How with magic there's nothing to fear. It is the essence of life itself." Her eyes hardened and her fingers curled into a fist. "The one thing that I regret is that I didn't know about it sooner. With wizardry, you have the possibility of even reliving your entire life. You could rewind time if you found the right spell."

Georgia scoffed. "I don't know about that."

"You don't?" Rose lifted a brow. "Then you should know. The potential for spells is limitless. There's no wall or barrier when it comes to what magic can do. Those of you who've lived with it your entire lives, you don't see that. You've been told that there is only so much that magic can give. But me? I see this very differently. I see that with power, real power, the world will open to you in the most beautiful of ways. You just have to be willing to jump when the time is right."

Her words made a lot of sense. Rose had much more passion for this than Georgia had ever expected. She thought Rose was simply an old secretary. She hadn't realized the depth of her love for magic.

"What would you do with it?" Georgia asked. "If you could work spells?"

Rose's eyes filled with whimsy. "I would ask for more time with my husband. That's all I want. Just a little more time. In some ways I suppose that I've gotten that, what with my learning about his secret life. But even that's no substitute for holding his hand again or even seeing his smiling face. I have plenty more years left. If I could only spend them with him, I'd be happy."

Georgia smiled warmly. Even though Rose was right about a lot of things, magic couldn't buy a person happiness. They had to find that within themselves. There were times when Georgia wished that she wasn't right about that, but it was the honest-to-goodness truth. Magic wasn't quite as limitless as Rose believed it to be. It was close, but there were still some things that magic couldn't do—like turn back time.

Because that's what Rose was asking for, a clock that she could rewind so that she'd be able to spend more moments with her husband.

Unfortunately it simply wasn't a possibility. But it would have been rude to say that. So Georgia slid her hand over Rose's soft one. "I hope that you get everything you wish for."

Rose smiled. "I do too, dear. I do, too."

CHAPTER 21

When Georgia went to get Judy from school that afternoon, she saw Missy in the pickup line. Missy waved to her and came over.

"Hey, Georgia, your costume is here. Want to come in and get it? It's in the library. Mrs. Roden has it."

Georgia inwardly groaned. "When is the book fair again?"

Missy pointed to the electronic sign. "In a few days."

Oh, crap. It sure was. How had time gotten away from Georgia? Easy. Her husband had almost died, they'd discovered that they had an orb that could raise crickets from the dead, and her sister might have breast cancer. She had a lot going on.

But instead of saying any of that, Georgia smiled. "Oh, okay. Right. Yes. Sorry. I've had a lot coming at me these past few days. I'll go in and get it."

The bell hadn't rung to dismiss the kids yet, so Georgia parked and headed inside to the library.

Mrs. Roden was there, in her office. Georgia knocked on the door and smiled. "I hear my cat costume is in."

Mrs. Roden, a petite thing with ebony curls and mahogany skin, smiled widely. "It sure is. You want to try it on and parade around in it for a few minutes?"

Georgia balked. "Um. Do I need to?"

"I'm just kidding. Let me get it to you." She pushed away from her desk and rummaged through boxes on the floor. "Here it is, the Candy the Cat costume."

Georgia took the box that she handed her. "Thanks."

"I know you might feel silly wearing it, but trust me, the kids are going to love it. They'll be so glad that this character has shown up that it'll be like seeing their favorite character at Disney World."

Somehow Georgia had the feeling that being a cat character from a book was in no way shape or form similar to seeing Goofy on Main Street, USA. But she didn't say anything to the contrary.

"I'll be sure to arrive in the costume. I'm looking forward to it," she lied.

Mrs. Roden swatted at her. "You don't have to lie. It's okay. You're doing us a big favor, and we appreciate it. But I tell you what, if you like the costume, you can always come to school on a regular day and show it off."

"Um…"

Mrs. Roden laughed. "Got you. Don't worry about it. But thank you."

Georgia took the costume and headed to Judy's classroom to grab her. As soon as she got Judy and was outside, her daughter asked about the box.

"What's in that, Mama?"

"Oh, just humiliation and embarrassment."

She cocked her chin. "What's humiliation?"

"Something I hope you don't learn about for a very, very long time."

"Okay," she said in a chipper voice.

Georgia laughed and she took Judy home and got dinner started. Dane returned from the gym, and they ate spaghetti and talked about their days.

"How did things go with Claudia?" he asked.

Georgia twirled saucy noodles around her fork. "It went great. We had a blast, and I got a couple of new outfits for myself."

"That's great. I can't wait to see them," he said, sounding more distracted than actually interested.

"Are you sure?" she questioned. "Because you don't sound that intrigued."

"No, I am," he told her, munching on his dinner. "I assure you that I am very interested in what you bought."

"Mama says she also bought humiliation," Judy announced.

Georgia felt her ears burn. "That's a little different, honey."

An amused smile crossed Dane's face. "Is it? Are you sure that you didn't buy humiliation at the unclaimed baggage place?"

"Oh, ha ha." She nearly tossed her napkin at him. "For your information, the humiliation has more to do with the giant cat suit that I have to wear at the book fair. That's where those feelings are coming from."

"You didn't have to volunteer," he reminded her.

"I know that but our school needed me to help out and what was I supposed to say?"

"No?"

She smirked. "Easy for you to do. You wouldn't have to deal with the wrath of Missy's angry looks every time you saw her, like I would have to deal with if I didn't volunteer."

"You're right about that," Dane said. "Seeing as how I don't even know her."

"See how lucky you are?" Georgia exhaled. The very movement made her deflate closer to her meal. "I'm the one who'll be in the cat suit and probably attacked by children who actually think I'm their cartoon cat hero."

"Let's not get ahead of ourselves," Dane said. "Let's take one thing at a time."

"Oh, okay. Let's," she said sarcastically.

"First, you'll be at the elementary school. I seriously doubt the children there will attack you."

"You don't know that," Georgia chirped. "They very well could go feral when they see me."

He rubbed his chin, his eyes twinkling with laughter. "Judy, do you think that Mommy is going to be attacked by children at the book fair?"

Red sauce was smeared all over her mouth. Judy wiped some of it off (streaking it more) as she considered Dane's question. "She might be attacked because aliens could show up."

Dane laughed. "See? Even Judy doesn't think that any bodily harm will happen to you from the children. She thinks it's all about the aliens."

"Both are possibilities," Georgia said flatly.

"I think both are not," Dane quipped. "My guess is that you'll be just fine on both counts. Now. I'll be happy to fit you into your costume and secure the back."

"It's not an evening dress," Georgia growled.

"It's really too bad that it's not. But I will help you. However I can."

"Do you want to wear it for me?" she asked eagerly.

"Um. No. Hon, I wish that I could. You know that I'd do anything for you. But the one thing I can't do is take your place when you've already signed up for something. What would Missy think if it was me in that costume and not you?"

"She would think that you're a super husband, that's what."

"But you and I would know the truth," he teased.

"That what? I randomly got sick at the last minute and you had to step in? Sounds like a plan if you ask me."

"No." He shook his head sharply. "We would both know that you weren't keeping your responsibilities like you promised to do for the PTO."

"I don't think that matters. The only thing that does is that there's a warm body inside that cat suit. That's it. It doesn't matter what the person looks like inside as long as they are at least over five feet tall."

"See? Then you win," Dane announced.

Georgia was barely over five feet. She didn't think that even at her height she was a good person for the suit. She would be a short cat. But Dane was not about to come to her rescue. Even though he wasn't saying it, he didn't want to be in the darned thing any more than she did.

"Well, I guess there's nothing I can do about it," Georgia said. "I'm going to be Candy the Cat no matter what."

"Mama, you're going to be the best Candy ever," Judy announced. "I'm going to tell all my friends, and we're going to come and give you big hugs. Will that make you feel better?"

Georgia laughed. "You know what, kiddo? It would make me feel a thousand times better. I would love that very much."

"Okay," Judy said as if it was completely settled.

"Okay," Georgia said with a laugh as she finished eating her spaghetti.

"See?" Dane said with a wink. "I knew it would all work out."

"No thanks to you," Georgia reminded him.

"This is a life lesson," he said with great satisfaction.

"What's a life lesson?" Judy asked.

Georgia replied, "Something that your dad thinks is important but really isn't."

Judy thought about that a minute and then said, "Okay."

They returned to their spaghetti and finished supper.

Half an hour later, Dane was helping Georgia with the dishes. "Are you upset?"

She rinsed a plate under hot water. "Why would I be upset?"

"Because you thought that I would take one for the team, but I won't."

"No, of course I'm not upset." She sighed. "I just wish that you *had* taken one for the team," she added with a smile.

"If it was something important, I would have."

"What's not important about wearing a cat suit?"

"So many things."

She laughed as Dane took a glass from her hands and dried it. "We have a meeting in a few minutes with Garryn."

Worry spiked down her spine. "What? At this time of night?"

Dane nodded. "We both need to talk to him, tell him what we've found. I vaguely briefed him this morning privately, and he wanted to talk about it after hours."

Georgia quirked a brow. "After hours? That sounds suspicious. Is everything okay?"

He shrugged. "I really don't know. But one thing I was going to ask is for the council to house the spell. I've done more research and am one hundred percent certain that it is a resurrection spell."

"Oh? And you want him to agree to this?"

"Exactly."

"But what about what Principal Brock said?"

Dane shook his head. "Even if that's true, that there's a traitor at the council, they have better security than we do. The spell will be safer there. Our family will be safer."

Georgia sighed but nodded in agreement. "Okay. I'm on board."

They finished the dishes, and Georgia checked on Judy, who was lying on their bed watching cartoons and coloring. "We're in the office if you need anything, honey."

"Okay, Mama," Judy replied.

Georgia shut the door and crossed into the office, where Dane was already setting up the laptop. "Ready to go?" she asked.

"Yep." He tapped a button, and the computer screen projected onto the wall. A moment later Garryn appeared. Behind him were several shelves of books. Georgia decided that he was in his home office as well.

"Thanks for meeting me tonight," the wizard councilman said.

"Of course." Dane sank into his office chair, and Georgia did the same—sat in hers, that was. "Is everything okay?"

A question that Georgia had as well. Why were they meeting so clandestine-like? Why couldn't they discuss business during the day? A strange feeling was crawling down her back. This was all very, very suspicious. Shouldn't the other council members hear what they had to talk about? Why was Garryn keeping information from them? The spaghetti, which had tasted so great going down, was creating a knot in her stomach.

"Everything's fine," he said with a smile. "I understand you have some sensitive information to tell me."

Dane spoke. "We think that we've discovered exactly what the two-toned orb does."

Garryn's brows shot to very interested peaks. "Really? I'd love to know."

Georgia took over. "We think it has the potential to raise the dead. We've seen this firsthand on insects. But we haven't tried it on anything else—like animals."

"But it's fair to say that if the orb works on one creature in that way, then it will work on others in the same manner," Dane said. "We watched it bring back dead corn as well. Then we moved on to insects."

Garryn rubbed his chin. "Intriguing. This is most unexpected. What else?"

Dane spoke. "We think that this is what the Gator is ultimately after —a weapon that can be used to raise the dead, possibly create an army of them. The implications for that would be huge. If a person could raise enough of the dead, then they could mobilize an entire army to do their bidding. They could overthrow governments, possibly even the world."

Garryn looked troubled. "Do you think?"

Dane continued. "We don't know the strength of the spell. What I mean by that is, even if you cut down someone who was already dead, would they return to dust or would they keep moving? How much damage do they have to take in order to be put back to pasture?"

"I see," Garryn murmured. "So we're in new territory."

"Exactly," Dane said. "But even though we're in this territory, we have to assume that Gator knows more about it than we do. He is, after all, the person who ordered Donalbain to search out the spell."

"That's true," Garryn mused. "So what do you want us to do now? What's your idea?"

"Well for one," Georgia said, "we need the spell to be kept under lock and key. We need it to be someplace safe."

"Someplace with security," Dane added. "More than what we have here."

Georgia lifted her brow at him to say, *What? You don't think that empty cans and string will keep the spell safe?*

Dane ignored the look she shot him. To Garryn he said, "We'd like to house the spell there, at the council headquarters."

Garryn grimaced. That was not the look that Georgia expected him to have. She expected some sort of childlike glee, some great look of confidence. She expected Garryn to open his arms and say, *Yes, give me the spell. I will use it for my evil machinations.*

Okay, perhaps she was going a little overboard in her thought processes. But it was safe to say that Garryn grimacing at them requesting that the council lock away the spell was not on the agenda.

The expression surprised her.

"Well," he said slowly, "we may have a bit of a problem there."

"How's that?" Dane asked.

Garryn tugged at the neck of his collar. "You see, it's come to my attention that there may be someone in the council who can't be trusted. I've gotten this from a reputable source. We have to be careful. If the wrong person discovered that the spell was here, I'm afraid that all could be lost. I'm sorry, but I cannot house the spell at the council. You'll have to keep it there, at your house."

CHAPTER 22

Georgia nearly fell out of her chair. Had she heard him right? Even Garryn was talking about a potential bad seed in the council?

Dane folded his arms, which made his biceps pop. That was definitely something that Georgia should not be noticing when she should have been paying attention to the news about the evil element on the council.

Her husband spoke. "Are you sure this isn't a rumor?"

What? Did he think that Principal Brock had been the one to tell Garryn about the baddie?

Garryn shook his head. "I'm afraid that what I've learned is much too coincidental to be a rumor. But I know without a doubt that since you have such a potentially dangerous orb of magic, that the best place for it is in your house, locked away."

"For how long?" Georgia asked. "The longer we keep it here, the more likely others are to discover what we have. This puts us at risk, too. Our daughter," she emphasized.

Garryn closed his eyes briefly. "I'm sorry. This isn't what I want to be asking of you. If it was up to me, I would tell you to bring the orb here. But trust me, it would be worse if we took the orb and it was stolen. The best thing for all of us right now is to hang tight."

Dane frowned. "This is powerful magic, Garryn. It can't be treated lightly."

He forced a smile. "That's why I'm glad it's in your hands. You will keep it safe. I know that. The two of you will do everything you can to keep it from the enemy. I wish that I could take it. It's what I want. But right now, as I've said, it's much too dangerous."

"How long?" Georgia asked, irritated. "How long will we have to keep it here?"

Yes, at first Georgia had thought that Garryn was suspicious, and she hadn't wanted to give him the orb. But the more he talked, the more she realized that he was being honest with them. He wasn't the Gator. If he was, he would've told them to drop the spell in his lap.

In answer to her question Garryn said, "I wish that I could tell you. Right now I'm just not sure. Maybe a few days. Maybe a week. But trust me, as soon as it's safe for the orb to leave your residence, I'll let you know."

She glanced over at Dane. "Looks like we have no choice but to store it."

Dane's jaw clenched. He wasn't happy with this, either. "Yep. Looks like. We'll just have to make sure that our security is as good as it can be."

Georgia nodded. "Okay, then."

They thanked Garryn, who apologized profusely for his inability to help them. Dane told him that it was okay, they understood.

Georgia begged to differ, but she kept her mouth shut. This was spilled milk if there ever was some. There was simply nothing they could do that would change the position that they had found themselves in.

"So," she said, turning to Dane. "Want to work on better booby traps for the house?"

He smirked. "Are you saying that you don't like the ones I made?"

"You mean the ones constructed of silly string and chewing gum? No. We need something better. Something that will actually do something."

"Mine did something," he countered. "I resent your suggestion that they didn't."

"If you consider catching a raccoon and our daughter's principal something, then I guess you're right. But I think we can do better."

He rolled his eyes.

She rose. "Come on. Let's work some real magic."

They put Judy to bed and then set up outside to create spells that would keep them safe. The first thing Georgia wanted to do was to create a barrier that would only allow in those who didn't want to harm them. It was a spell created of pure intention and would teach them a lot about who their friends were. Of that she was certain.

She took a green orb of protection and squashed it between her hands. An emerald light split out from her palms. Georgia gestured up, telling the light where she wanted it to go. The orb made a dome over the house and blinked one time before a suctioning sound came from the ground, suggesting that the spell was active.

"Show-off," Dane grumbled.

She smiled brightly. "You could have just as easily created that. We have plenty of protection spells."

"I prefer doing things my way."

"Right. With chewing gum."

"I resent that."

She shrugged. "What else do we want?"

"Another spell over the door where the basement is," he told her.

Right. If someone managed to get through the first spell, then a secondary one would be needed to stop a trespasser farther.

They went inside, and she grabbed a sealing spell from the basement. She squished the orb against the doorframe. Pink ooze ran down the wood like slime.

She focused her intention and told the spell that only Dane and she were allowed down the stairs. That was it. No one else. The slime worked its way like a slug to the floor and then back up, making a rectangle.

"Why are your spells so strange looking?" Dane asked.

She shot him a scathing look. "Because they work."

"Let's hope so."

"They will," she told him.

If there was one thing that Georgia used to be good at, it was protection spells. Dane just didn't happen to know that about her because he had never bothered to ask.

But anyway, when she finished sealing the door to the basement, Georgia brushed her hands. "Okay. I believe that should do it. What do you think?"

Dane nodded. "It'll do for now."

"For now?"

"We may end up wanting an extra protection spell or two. Let's see how we feel in the morning."

"I know how I'll feel."

"How's that?"

"Protected," she snapped.

His dark eyes twinkled with amusement. "Okay, you've got me. Come on. Let's go to bed."

Now that, Georgia could agree to. They changed their clothes and brushed their teeth. As they slipped under the covers, Georgia snuggled up to Dane.

"I love you," she murmured.

He brushed his lips across her forehead. "I love you more."

"Okay," she joked. "I'll accept that."

He snapped off the light, and within minutes Georgia had drifted off into a dreamless sleep.

CHAPTER 23

Things remained quiet the next few days at the Nocturne household. The spells that Georgia had created held, and life seemed to get back into somewhat of a normal routine. They didn't hear any chatter over the airwaves about Gator, and for that, Georgia was grateful.

She still sat on pins and needles awaiting Claudia's results, which should literally have been in any hour. She kept looking at her phone expectantly, and whenever it chirped or even looked like it was going to make a sound, Georgia had it in her hand, checking to see if Claudia had buzzed her.

But no such luck.

The day of the book fair arrived, and so did Georgia's grand humiliation. She was all set to head over to the fair after dinner, though she would have preferred dressing up like the cat during the morning, when she figured less parents would be around.

Not that she thought any of the parents would judge her. Of course they wouldn't judge her. It was simply that dressing up like a cat was, well, you know…humiliating.

But she wiggled into the costume after dinner. It was decidedly hot. There was no room for argument. As soon as she had the heavy material over her shoulders, her back started sprouting with sweat. She still wore a shirt and jeans under the thing, but that would have to change.

So Georgia peeled off the costume and put on a workout shirt with a racer back and a pair of shorts. When she pulled the costume back on, she wasn't sweating an ocean of water anymore, but it was still hot, just not Dante's *Inferno* hot.

"You all set?" Dane asked, walking into the bedroom. He saw her, did a double take, stopped and brought a hand to his lips in admiration. "Wow. I have to say that you look—"

"If you like having all your male parts, you won't say another word."

"I do like having all of them."

"Then you will be quiet."

"But all I was going to say is that you look charming."

She stared at herself in the mirror. She had a big red body with a fuzzy peach oval-shaped stomach. There was nothing cute about it.

"I don't even have my head on."

"I kind of like that you're half-human, half-animal. It's different."

She rolled her eyes. "You're being silly. Are you ready to head out?"

"I don't know. Are you?" he joked.

"I am seriously going to do you bodily harm if you don't stop teasing me."

"Okay." He lifted his hands in surrender, but that sneaky smile stayed on his face. "I will stop teasing you. Now, where's your head so that we can get going?"

She pointed to it. "It's in the chair. Can you bring it for me?"

"Of course." He turned toward the door. "Judy! You ready?"

Judy bounded into the room. She took one look at Georgia and squealed. "You look great, Mama!" She raced over and threw her arms around Georgia's waist. "You make a great cat."

"Thank you, sweetheart."

"See?" Dane said. "I told you the same thing."

"Yes, you sure did. Now. Can we go?"

Dane looked at Judy and Judy grinned. "We're ready, Mama."

"Okay, let's head out."

When they reached the school, Georgia put on her head—literally. The giant cat head was heavy and didn't have a good center of gravity. The majority of its weight was in the back so Georgia had to work to keep her head straight and prayed she wouldn't suffer from whiplash in the morning.

"How long do I have to do this?" she muttered.

"Let's hope only thirty minutes," Dane told her. "Come on. Let's go to the library."

It was still a few minutes before all the kids showed up. The library was decorated beautifully with loads of books everywhere and colorful streamers. There were tons of things for the kids to buy, and when Mrs. Roden saw Georgia, she spread out her hands and smiled.

"Why, you look beautiful," she said cheerfully.

"Thank you," was all Georgia said. Though she was tempted to add that if she fell over it would be because the head pulled her to the floor with its massive weight.

"I just want you to wander around," Mrs. Roden said. "How's that sound?"

"Do I get a handler?" she asked.

Mrs. Roden laughed. It wasn't funny to Georgia. In Disney all the characters always got handlers, people ready to punch anyone who was belligerent enough to get too close to Mickey Mouse. If Mickey had a handler, didn't a giant cat need one, too?

"I'll be your handler," Dane said. "I'll make sure that everyone treats you with the respect that you deserve."

"Oh, thank you," Georgia said, relieved. "Great."

Mrs. Roden clasped her hands. "Well, that's all settled. Oh, looks like my volunteers are here. I need to teach them how to use the cash registers. We'll open in a few minutes."

As soon as the main doors to the library opened about ten minutes later, kids and parents came streaming into the book fair, and half of them made a beeline straight for Georgia.

She felt her entire body bow in as a dozen snot-clinging-to-noses kids scrambled to get close to her.

"It's Candy," one boy said.

A little girl pressed her face against Georgia's arm. "Oh, kitty, I love you."

"Is there a person inside?" A boy knocked on her head. "There's a person in there. I can see you! I can see her," he told other kids.

Dane jumped in. "Now, everybody, let's be nice to the cat. The kitty's here to see everyone and to take pictures. Now. Who wants a photo?"

"Me," several kids yelled.

So Dane spent the next half an hour placing Georgia with kids so that their parents could get photos of them together. Once Dane was in control and getting the pictures done, the children stopped pawing at her for the most part.

For the most part.

There were still some who tried to see her eyes and who rapped on her head. On every knock it felt like her head was going to sling off, but somehow Georgia managed to keep it on.

Don't ask her how she did it. It must've been a miracle.

They were in about an hour deep when Dane's phone rang. He glanced down at the screen and frowned. "Be right back," he said before disappearing and leaving her to the mob of children.

The kids didn't take her down to the ground, which she was elated about. Georgia managed to hold her own as she watched Dane wander off into a corner of the room, a deep wrinkle of concern indented in his forehead.

She remembered seeing that line a long time ago, when they were first getting to know one another, and loving it at first sight. You know, there were just some people who made worrying look sexy, and Dane was one of them. He could make worry, even guilt look good enough to eat.

But even as she watched his look of complete uncertainty as he listened to whoever was on the phone, Georgia couldn't bring herself to find any lightness in the moment. As if he knew that she was thinking about him, Dane made eye contact with her and then quickly glanced away, turning to face the corner.

Kids were pulling on her now, so she directed her attention back to them, waving and putting one hand on her hip, or wrapping an arm around a child's shoulders for a picture.

Even though it was hot in the costume, it felt as if her internal furnace had just been put on inferno. Sweat poured down her forehead and slicked her palms. Georgia knew that it was stress from whoever Dane was talking to more than it was the actual temperature inside the suit.

He never would've taken a call in the middle of the book fair unless it had been super important, and he wouldn't have his back turned away from her, masking his response, unless whatever the news was, it was super bad.

So she was quietly freaking out while still managing to pose for pictures.

Finally, after what literally seemed like forever, Dane ended the call and strode back over to her, his mouth in a tight grimace and his feet hitting the floor with such force that Georgia was surprised that books weren't falling from the shelves.

"What was that about?" she asked before he could say a word.

"That was Garryn."

"Everything okay?"

She knew it was a stupid question before it even left her mouth. Of course everything was not okay. Dane had just spent five minutes in a corner.

He shook his head. "We need to leave."

"Leave, now? Why?" The hairs on the back of her neck bristled to attention. "How bad is it?"

His eyes darkened. "It's very bad."

A knot clogged up her throat. "How bad?"

His brow furrowed, and Dane nearly growled, "It's Donalbain. He's escaped."

The floor fell away. The library began to spin. Georgia inhaled sharply, doing what she could to keep from losing control. "Do they know where he's gone?"

"They have a theory."

"Where?"

"Our house. To get that spell."

CHAPTER 24

They grabbed Judy and rushed home. They didn't have any options, really. There wasn't anyone at the school that they could leave their daughter with, so taking her home seemed like the best option.

Besides, Dane and Georgia were both spell hunters. They could fight off just about anything.

When they reached their house, it was eerily quiet. Dane had called Brad on their way, letting him know what was going on. Brad said that he would be right over.

"Be careful," Brad had said over the Bluetooth speaker.

"You too," Dane said. "We don't know where exactly Donalbain is heading. He could be coming toward us. He could be headed toward you, thinking that you know something. We all must be on alert."

They hung up, and from the back seat Judy said, "Mama, is everything okay?"

Georgia twisted around as best she could seeing as she was still wearing the cat suit. "Yes. It's all going to be okay. But Daddy and I need you to listen to us very carefully. Everything we tell you to do, we need you to do it. Okay? Do you understand?"

"Yes, I understand."

"Okay, great."

They reached the house, and Dane hit the button to open the garage door. The car slipped inside, and he shut off the vehicle. The only sound was the ticking of the engine as it came to a stop.

"Let's get inside and check the spell," Georgia said.

They climbed out, and Georgia hoisted the cat head under her arm. The house still seemed too quiet, but she had pulsed her magic when they'd gone under the protection spells. They were holding strong.

When they reached the kitchen, Georgia put Candy's head on a table, and Dane tromped down into the basement.

A moment later he shouted, "Georgia! Get down here!"

That was his somebody's-in-trouble voice. What could possibly have Dane all riled up?

When she got downstairs, she saw what the commotion was about. The spell, the resurrection spell, as it was, sat in the mason jar as it had, but surrounding it were about thirty other spells exactly like it—clones of the original.

"What in the world?" she mused.

Dane shot her a dark look. "Exactly. What have you been doing?"

"What do you mean, what have I been doing? I haven't been doing anything."

"Well, somebody had to have cloned all these. I didn't do it."

She bristled. "Don't look at me. I had nothing to do with this."

They stared at each other, and at the same time a lightbulb went off inside their heads. "Judy," they whispered simultaneously.

"Judy, would you please come down here?" Dane called.

Judy climbed down the stairs. "Yes, Daddy." Her gaze fell on the scores of orbs flitting dangerously about the room. "Oh," she whispered. Her face crumpled. "I'm sorry, Daddy. I didn't mean to. I was just playing."

Georgia's jaw fell. Judy had been going into the basement without them knowing. It had been *her* the day of the barbecue who'd left the door open when Garryn had wound up downstairs. And the spell that Judy had used to seal the door, that only Georgia or Dane could enter—well, the spell must've picked up some of Georgia and Dane in Judy. She was their child, after all.

But copying the spell?

Dane crouched in front of her. "How did you do it?"

"I saw the liquid that you made. The blue stuff, there." She pointed to the vial. "It copies. I can see that. So I poured some in and asked it to work fast."

"You asked it to work fast?" Georgia asked, astonished.

"Uh-huh."

There had been one clone and the original that Dane had left in the mason jar. Their daughter had made copies for fun—and she'd made the spell work faster! She was brilliant. Or highly dangerous. Georgia didn't know which, but thought it safe to assume that the answer was possibly both.

"Oh, wow," Dane said tightly. "Honey, if you're going to play with spells, you need to let us know, okay?"

Judy's face crumpled. "Did I do something bad?"

"No, no. Not at all. You are fine. But sometimes spells may not be so friendly. They could cause problems. So please, the safest thing to do is to leave all of them alone. Okay?"

"Am I in trouble?" she asked, though it sounded a bit like begging.

"No, no, honey. Not at all." Dane hugged her close. "You're not in trouble."

While he was consoling Judy, Georgia started quickly plucking the spells from the air and storing them in another mason jar. She managed to get the spells inside, stuffing them way down until they were squeezed in like sardines. She screwed the lid on just as a loud crash came from upstairs.

Dane and Georgia said simultaneously, "Donalbain."

Dane handed Judy off to her and charged upstairs. "Stay here, Judy," she said. "I want you to hide in the deepest corner you can and stay out of sight, okay?"

Her eyes brimmed with tears. "Will I be okay?"

"Yes, yes, honey. You're going to be fine. Just do what I say. All right?"

Judy nodded and Georgia gently pushed her toward a corner. "Don't come out until either me or Daddy tell you it's safe. Okay?"

"Okay," she murmured.

Since Donalbain was there to retrieve the spells, Georgia grabbed the mason jar that was chock-full of them and stuffed it down her cat costume. Yes. She was still wearing it.

With the jar tucked safely in her waist, she charged up the stairs and slammed the door shut behind her. She didn't have to go far to hear Dane and Donalbain squabbling.

Their front door stood wide open. Donalbain was just outside it, hovering in the air. A weirdly strange blue light haloed him (again) as if he'd brought his own movie lighting designer to make sure that he looked wicked and scary.

"Ah, I see the wife has made it." His gaze washed up and down her outfit. "I must've interrupted the two of you in the middle of a tryst. I didn't realize that you were into the whole fuzzy costume thing."

Georgia rolled her eyes. "You managed to escape jail, but you are not going to get your hands on that spell, Donalbain."

Dane glanced over at her. "I already told him that. He didn't listen to me, and I pretty much doubt that he's going to listen to you."

"Rude," Georgia said with a scoff. "I don't understand why he wouldn't listen to you. Or me. I guess it doesn't matter. He's not even going to get inside of this house."

Donalbain glanced up at the doorway and smirked. "I don't need to get inside. I am the messenger of Gator. He has made sure that my escape came true. I will get the orb, and I will be free and make his will happen!"

"Wow," Georgia said to Dane. "He's really got quite the ego."

Dane nodded. "I agree."

Donalbain clenched his fists. "Will you two shut up?"

Before they could get out a word otherwise, he hit them with a blast of magic. In order to avoid being speared, Dane and Georgia darted in opposite directions.

The blast of power hit their doorstep, sending bricks flying.

Dane yelled, "Our insurance isn't going to pay for that."

"Luckily we have magic to fix it," Georgia called.

Donalbain shouted, "I will get you!"

He threw magic at Dane, who tossed power right back at him. Their streams of magic clashed half the distance between them.

What were the neighbors going to think?

Needing to stop this mess before it got out of hand, Georgia raised her palm and threw magic at Donalbain.

But Donalbain's head whipped in her direction. The hand not shooting power at Dane rose, and a line headed straight for her.

She didn't have time to dodge it. Georgia froze like a deer in headlights. Then all of a sudden, she was being thrown to the ground.

"Ugh." Her adrenaline was kicking in, but that did not stop the pain that ratcheted up her back. "Good Lord, I am too old for this crap."

"Georgia, do you have the spell?"

Garryn stood off to the side, his hands out. He looked worried, and hurried.

She rubbed her head. A knot was forming from where she'd hit the ground. Her gaze swished to Donalbain. Dane was still fighting with him, and it didn't look like either one of them was winning.

"What?" was all she could think to say.

"The spell," Garryn insisted. "Give it to me now. I'll get it out of here so that Donalbain doesn't get ahold of it."

Wait. Weren't they supposed to be keeping it? That knot was really doing a number on her noggin. "But what about the bad councilman?"

"I know who it is. I can keep it away from him. Now. Give me the spell so that you can stop Donalbain. Dane's having a hard time over there."

A quick look told her that Dane was holding his own, but he could use backup. She needed to get in there and give him whatever support she could. Which meant handing the spells over to Garryn. That was okay, wasn't it? He was on their side, right? That's what Dane had been telling her for days. It was high time that Georgia just decided to go ahead and trust Garryn. Give him the spell. It would be easy. Just take them out of her cat suit and throw the spells over.

But still, there was a desperation in his expression that Georgia hadn't seen before. It worried her, sent a shudder straight to her core.

"Please, Georgia," he pleaded. "We don't have a lot of time. Give me the spell."

Dane yelled and Donalbain was encroaching on him. There wasn't any time left. She had to help her husband. Without thinking, Georgia pulled the spells from her huge cat suit and tossed the mason jar at Garryn.

"Here! Take them!"

His eyes flared with delight as he glimpsed the spells sailing toward him. He caught them in one hand and lifted the glass high, shaking it.

"Now I've got it! I have the power to do whatever I want!"

What? Was this guy suddenly going to lift his sword to the sky and turn into He-Man? And where was Skeletor?

A sick feeling spread across Georgia's stomach. "Please don't tell me that I made a mistake."

He flashed a grin. "Okay, I won't. But you have."

"You." Her fingers curled into fists. "You're the Gator."

"Me?" Garryn chuckled. "Hardly. I'm not the Gator. But I work for him, and he will reward me highly when he gets ahold of these resurrection spells."

"You lied to us." She swore. "I knew that you couldn't be trusted, but Dane told me that I was being silly. That you were a good person."

Garryn swept a hand over his head, smoothing his hair. "You shouldn't have listened to your husband."

"I knew it."

"Now I'm afraid that I must be going," he said casually, as if they were at a party and it was time for his exit. "But it's been great doing business with you."

"Oh no you don't!"

Garryn turned to leave, and Georgia shot him with a wave of magic. He whipped to face her and smiled petulantly before opening his hand and absorbing her power.

"I learned a few tricks from my friend Donalbain," he sneered. "Don't fight me. You won't win."

"You're not going to steal those spells and use them to create an army of the dead!"

"Not me, Gator. But it's not my worry what happens with them. I'm only the delivery man. Gator's the real mastermind."

Tired of hearing him talk about Gator, Georgia threw another line of magic at Garryn, who sucked it into him again. "Keep pushing me, Georgia, and you won't like how this turns out."

"I'll push you as hard as I can. You will give me back that jar."

"Over my dead body," he growled.

Fine by her. First and foremost, Georgia's responsibility was to making sure the magic didn't get into the wrong hands. But Garryn was proving difficult to fight. If she kept hitting him with magic and he continued to store her power, eventually he would hit her with a blast that could kill her.

Hmm. She needed a workaround. Thinking fast, she aimed her magic at an oak tree over Garryn's head. A spear of power blasted onto a branch, severing it from the trunk. It fell straight down, aiming for Garryn's head.

He saw the branch just in time and charged to the side. Georgia only had to hope that his grip on the spells had loosened a tiny bit.

She created a lasso of magic and threw it onto the jar, ensnaring it. With one quick tug the glass and spells were safely back in her hands.

Garryn whirled on her. "You're going to regret that."

It was definitely a possibility, but Georgia hoped not. Power built up around Garryn. He was doing exactly what Georgia had hoped that he wouldn't—he was charging up all that magic that she had thrown at him.

She glanced over at Dane, but he was still entangled with Donalbain. Seriously? How had her husband not defeated him by now?

To save herself, Georgia quickly created a shield right before Garryn blasted her with magic. It was a rod of power, a tunnel of it aimed straight at her.

Magic poured into her shield. The force of it pushed her back. Georgia held hard, giving the barrier more magic, but Garryn was stronger. Figured.

He didn't have to get a five-year-old up and ready for school every day. He didn't have to spend an hour in the kitchen every night whipping up a dinner that his family may or may not like. He didn't have to make sure the house was clean every day and wipe down the toilets.

No. Probably all Garryn had to do was work his nine-to-five and then mow the lawn on the weekends.

Well, Georgia had to work her nine-to-whenever and still manage to run a house and keep everyone in it alive.

That was true stress.

But right now, even with her extra anger fuel, Garryn was still winning. His magic was beginning to tunnel a hole into her shield. She couldn't keep it solid for much longer.

Georgia hunkered down and poured more power into it. But a surge of magic pulsed in his hands. The strength of it was more than Georgia expected, and it blew her back into their bushes.

She was pretty sure the entire neighborhood would be out of their houses any second to see exactly what was going on. She could just hear them murmuring to themselves, wondering why someone was lighting fireworks. It wasn't even the Fourth of July.

Her vision was fuzzy on the edges as Garryn approached. "I told you to give me the spells. If only you had just listened in the first place. Now I'll have to kill you and your husband."

"No," she said weakly.

The blast had zapped more of her strength than she had originally thought. She lifted her hand to stop Garryn as he charged his magic and released a blast right in her face.

Then he was sailing through the sky and landing about ten feet back.

"What?" she whispered, figuring Dane had come to her rescue.

But it was not Dane. Standing in what she could only describe as a superhero leotard stood Principal Brock.

He had on a mask so that regular people wouldn't recognize him, but his glasses gave him away.

"Who are you?" Garryn asked.

"I'm the Grim Reaper," Stan Brock said. "Be prepared to meet your match."

Garryn started to laugh but Stan flung out his hand and Garryn went slack. He then whipped toward Donalbain and did the same thing. Donalbain immediately stopped throwing magic at Dane and slumped to the ground.

Georgia scrambled to her feet. "What did you do?"

Stan blew on his fingertips. "Just knocked them out so that you can have them arrested. Don't worry, I didn't use my full-on grim power. Just enough to sedate them."

Dane extended his hand. "Thank you. I never thought I was going to get out of that."

"Me neither," Georgia said before pointing to Garryn. "I told you about him."

Dane looked sheepish. "Yes, you did. I should have listened."

Stan placed his fists on his hips. "I'm just glad that I got here in time."

"How'd you know that we needed help?"

He pressed a finger to his nose. "Simple. I saw y'all leave the book fair."

"That sounds about right," Georgia said.

Just then, two cars pulled up. Georgia scanned the road, and sure enough, some folks had come out of their homes and had witnessed the event.

Brad jumped out of his SUV and ran down. "Everything okay?"

Dane shook his head. "We'll need to contact the council and tell them that Garryn was dirty. He was working with Donalbain, and I believe he's the Gator."

"No, he isn't," Georgia corrected. "He told me that himself."

Dane looked perplexed. "Well, even so. We need to get them gone."

Brad thumbed toward the folks on the road. "What about them?"

Georgia grimaced. "Memory-swipe time?"

Dane nodded. "I'll get the spell."

Claudia emerged from the second car and rushed down. "Georgia, is everything okay?"

"It's fine." Fear raced down her spine at the sight of her sister looking frantic. "What about you? Are you okay?"

"Yes, the hospital called and left a message. I only just heard it and came over to tell you."

Georgia was afraid to ask. "Well? What did they say?"

Claudia flung her arms around her sister. "It's benign. I'm okay! They took extra long in telling me because they were looking at several samples and wanted to make sure that there wasn't one trace of cancer in any of them. That's why the tests took longer than normal."

Georgia hugged her sister tight. "What great news."

Dane cleared his throat. "How about we get this mess cleared up?"

Georgia glanced at the folks watching and the bodies on the ground. They'd better do something before a nosy neighbor decided to call the police. "Yes, let's."

CHAPTER 25

Georgia and Dane got everyone's memory swiped, and both Donalbain and Garryn were thrown into jail at the wizard council. At least, that's what they were told.

Georgia was apt to be skeptical. Dane believed it, though he did apologize for not listening to her gut when she told him that Garryn was slimy.

He started making it up to her by entering their bedroom the next morning with breakfast in bed and then taking Judy to school.

It was a start, Georgia figured.

By the time he returned, Brad and Rose had arrived and they were getting ready to sit down at their morning meeting.

"Well, I heard you had quite the night," Rose said.

Georgia nodded. "We sure did, and thanks to Judy's principal, Stan Brock, we all survived it."

"Oh my, I'm sorry that it was so touch and go," Rose murmured.

"The important thing," Dane said, "is that Garryn and Donalbain have been locked up. We know that it was Garryn who released Donalbain to begin with, so that he could get his hands on the resurrection spell."

"Of which there are like a thousand of them now," Georgia said.

His gaze darted to her. "But we've hidden them in a safe place. This morning, after I dropped Judy off, I put the spells in a spot where no one will find them."

"It sounds like a good thing for everyone," Rose replied happily. "After all, we can't have anyone getting their hands on that spell." She paused. "Do you happen to know who the Gator is, by the way?"

Dane shook his head. "No, we never did figure that out. Garryn and Donalbain claim not to know."

"Whoever he is," Brad started, "the guy's elusive. Let me tell you."

"He sure is," Dane seconded. "But if we put our heads together, I'm sure that we can come up with the riddle of who he is."

"Let's hope so," Brad said. "Because he's recruiting anyone he can for his dirty work."

"We may need more good guys on our side," Georgia said.

Everyone agreed. A little while later they broke for lunch. Brad and Rose went out to pick up some Chinese food. When they were alone, Georgia said to Dane, "So where exactly did you hide the spells?"

"I dug a hole in the forest and buried them there. They aren't around a graveyard or any place where if they get loose, they'll be able to bring back anyone who's dead."

"Well, that's a relief."

His lips quirked into a crooked grin. "Did you actually think that I would place the spells someplace where they could easily be discovered?"

"No, of course not." She pressed her lips to his. "I know that you'll protect us better than that."

He pulled away and brushed a hand through his hair. "I just hope that I can keep protecting us. We've got to find out who the Gator is. While he's out there, none of us are safe."

She nodded absently. Dane was right. But there wasn't time to ponder it because their doorbell rang. She shot him a confused look. "You expecting anyone?"

He shook his head. "You?"

"No."

She crossed to the front of the house. When she opened the door, there stood Principal Brock, glasses high on his nose, legs splayed wide.

He gave her a toothy grin. "I've come to join the team."

"Join the team?" she said, unable to hide her surprise.

"If you'll have me, that is. The way I see it, I could be an asset—after everything that happened last night, that is."

Georgia thought about it. Stan had helped them. In fact, he'd saved her life. A slow smile spread across her face, and she opened the door wider. "Rose and Brad just left to pick up Chinese, but I can call them with an extra order. What would you like to eat?"

∽

Thank you for reading SPELL STRUCK. I hope you enjoyed it.

Never miss a release! Be sure to sign up for my newsletter so that you're up to date on all my news. Click HERE to sign up!

Plus, join my private Facebook group, the Bless Your Witch Club. There you will receive sneak peaks at books, be the first to receive special giveaway offers and watch as I interview other authors that you love. But it's only available in the club, so join HERE.

And…I love to hear from you! Please feel free to drop me a line anytime. You can email me amy@amyboylesauthor.com.

ALSO BY AMY BOYLES

SERIES READING ORDER

MIDLIFE SPELL HUNTER
SPELL HUNTER
SPELL STRUCK
SPELL CAST (Coming early 2022)

A MAGICAL RENOVATION MYSERY
WITCHER UPPER
RENOVATION SPELL
DEMOLITION PREMONITION
WITCHER UPPER CHRISTMAS
BARN BEWITCHMENT
SHIPLAP AND SPELL HUNTING
MUDROOM MYSTIC
WITCH IT OR LIST IT

LOST SOUTHERN MAGIC
(Sweet Tea Witches, Southern Belles and Spells, Southern Ghost Wrangles and Bless Your Witch Crossover)
THE GOLD TOUCH THAT WENT CATTYWAMPUS
THE YELLOW-BELLIED SCAREDY CAT
A MESS OF SIRENS
KNEE-HIGH TO A THIEF

BELLES AND SPELLS MATCHMAKER MYSTERY
DEADLY SPELLS AND A SOUTHERN BELLE
CURSED BRIDES AND ALIBIS
MAGICAL DAMES AND DATING GAMES

SOME PIG AND A MUMMY DIG

SWEET TEA WITCH MYSTERIES
SOUTHERN MAGIC
SOUTHERN SPELLS
SOUTHERN MYTHS
SOUTHERN SORCERY
SOUTHERN CURSES
SOUTHERN KARMA
SOUTHERN MAGIC THANKSGIVING
SOUTHERN MAGIC CHRISTMAS
SOUTHERN POTIONS
SOUTHERN FORTUNES
SOUTHERN HAUNTINGS
SOUTHERN WANDS
SOUTHERN CONJURING
SOUTHERN WISHES
SOUTHERN DREAMS
SOUTHERN MAGIC WEDDING
SOUTHERN OMENS
SOUTHERN JINXED
SOUTHERN BEGINNINGS
SOUTHERN MYSTICS
SOUTHERN CAULDRONS

SOUTHERN GHOST WRANGLER MYSTERIES
SOUL FOOD SPIRITS
HONEYSUCKLE HAUNTING
THE GHOST WHO ATE GRITS (Crossover with Pepper and Axel from Sweet Tea Witches)
BACKWOODS BANSHEE
MISTLETOE AND SPIRITS

BLESS YOUR WITCH SERIES

SCARED WITCHLESS

KISS MY WITCH

QUEEN WITCH

QUIT YOUR WITCHIN'

FOR WITCH'S SAKE

DON'T GIVE A WITCH

WITCH MY GRITS

FRIED GREEN WITCH

SOUTHERN WITCHING

Y'ALL WITCHES

HOLD YOUR WITCHES

SOUTHERN SINGLE MOM PARANORMAL MYSTERIES

The Witch's Handbook to Hunting Vampires

The Witch's Handbook to Catching Werewolves

The Witch's Handbook to Trapping Demons

ABOUT THE AUTHOR

Hey, I'm Amy,

I write books for folks who crave laugh-out-loud paranormal mysteries. I help bring humor into readers' lives. I've got a Pharm D in pharmacy, a BA in Creative Writing and a Masters in Life.

And when I'm not writing or chasing around two small children (one of which is four going on thirteen), I can be found antique shopping for a great deal, getting my roots touched up (because that's an every four week job) and figuring out when I can get back to Disney World.

If you're dying to know more about my wacky life, here are three things you don't know about me.

—In college I spent a semester at Marvel Comics working in the X-Men office.

—I worked at Carnegie Hall.

—I grew up in a barbecue restaurant—literally. My parents owned one.

If you want to reach out to me—and I love to hear from readers—you can email me at amyboylesauthor@gmail.com.

Happy reading!

Manufactured by Amazon.ca
Bolton, ON